Early Yet

Early Yet

Seven Short Stories
and a Novella by

Frank Soos

St. Andrews College Press
Laurinburg, North Carolina
1998

Acknowledgments:

"The Other Side of Christiansburg": *Mississippi Valley Review*
"Two O' Clock in the Afternoon": *The Crescent Review*
"Three Weird Things": *Gargoyle*
"Star Drill": *Sonora Review*
"Weasel's Daddy": *O. Henry Festival Stories*
"Jackson of All Trades": *Writers' Forum*
"Roland Barker and his Red Guitar": *Quarterly West*

Library of Congress Cataloging-in-Publication Data

Soos, Frank 1950. Early yet / Frank Soos—
Laurinburg, NC / St. Andrews College Press
        I. Soos, Frank. II. Title

St. Andrews College Press
1700 Dogwood Mile
Laurinburg, NC 28352

Cover design: Ron Rozzelle

ISBN: 1-879934-52-3

Typeset in Berkeley Oldstyle Book

First Printing: January 1998

Contents

Star Drill   1

Monkeys   12

Jackson of All Trades   22

Three Weird Things   32

Two O'Clock in the Afternoon   52

The Other Side of Christiansburg   59

Weasel's Daddy   74

Roland Barker and his Red Guitar   89

To the memory of my father,
Frank M. Soos
1921-1997

Star Drill

Out on the court they are doing the star drill, with the first five on one end and the rest on the other. It used to be my favorite drill—one girl shoots from the corners, the wings, the top of the key while the others take the rebounds and throw them back to her. Only with me there weren't any rebounds, or hardly any. I could move from corner to corner on the five pointed star and back again without missing. I was what Poppa Bear called a pure shooter, though I had my bad nights, too. Now I am in the roll-out bleachers watching and waiting for practice to be over so I can talk to Poppa Bear.

Poppa Bear, so fat that it puts him out of breath to walk the length of the gym floor, is down with the subs, showing them the tricks of shooting the ball like a boy—how to hold the ball in one hand and let it go with the other, pointing the middle finger at where you want the ball to go, shooting for the glass like they always did at UCLA when Johnny Wooden was their coach. Down at this end the girls under the basket talk about boys and clothes and their mothers, of course, but the star drill goes on. If you haven't learned that by now, you aren't going to be out on the floor for Poppa Bear.

Which is why I need to talk to him. My own daddy who sold cars (used) sometimes and insurance others and who read the paper and said, "Un hun, yes, just a minute," was just a ghost in the house. And Mother who mainly was nag, nag,

1

nag, and more, more, more, looked mostly after her wardrobe instead of me. She spent her time at shoe sales or in front of the mirror fixing her face. When I started playing ball, she was against it, but liked it after I started getting in the *Tribune*. Still she said, "It's ruining you, making your legs look all out of proportion." Daddy came to a game once; "Very interesting," he said.

So should it be surprising that when the guidance counselor took me into the office and said what about my future, I just looked out the window at the not so busy street. "Well," she wondered out loud about college and whether I should go and what were my interests, paused a while expecting me to chime in with how I just loved this or that, then said, "I can't believe you haven't any interests," in her not I-know-so-much way. I just looked like who was she, and then she said maybe I might find myself in the Service. "The Service," that was the word she used, and it took me a minute to figure out that she was talking about the Army. Maybe I shouldn't have laughed. How could I tell her I had it in my head what I wanted to do—to be the first girl who played for Poppa Bear to score over a thousand points. After that, we would see what came next.

There was Randy Cobb, of course. He wasn't much thought of by Mother who just said, "What you see in him I'll never know." He had this way of rearing back in his desk and stretching, wore cowboy boots, owned a horse and a Ford Fairlane with a tape deck. He was all right, good looking and strong. And everybody said he could've done something in football if he'd ever stayed out for the team. I'll admit I liked him because he was strong, because when he held me when we wrestled just playing or fought for real, I knew I was being held.

Poppa Bear tried to break us up, but I never held that against him. He did it to all the girls—anything was fair to him if it was for the good of the team. On short winter days when we were still practicing way past dark, Poppa Bear would walk to the windows in the lobby of the gym, and if he saw Randy Cobb, or anybody else for that matter, but it was usually Randy, sitting out in the driveway with his engine running, he would come back in the gym and give us extra foul shots or suicides or figure eights and fast breaks until Randy got pissed off and left. Then I would have to walk with the wind blowing up my skirt to the phone booth outside Snow's Grocery Store and call Randy at home, where he wasn't and then at the Rec Hall, where he had gone to shoot pool and forget about anything we had planned for the night. He would make me apologize and beg, knowing it wasn't my fault. And like a dummy, I would do it. I don't know why except that finally getting him to come get me out of that cold phone booth made me feel like I'd done something, like maybe I really did count with somebody, even if it was Randy Cobb.

He would give me beer, but I would take only one because I had read somewhere that pro football players had one a day, and it was good for them. And we'd go to the Tastee Freeze where I would pig out on hamburgers, french fries and all the rest; I could eat like that all day then except when we lost. Then I couldn't keep anything down until after the next day's practice. When, after running and running all the full court drills ever invented, we would have to run a suicide for every free throw missed the night before, for every bad pass, until I, having had nothing really to eat for almost twenty-four hours would be dizzy and ready to faint. It was a good thing we hardly ever lost.

Then Randy and me would go out to the lake and get in the back seat with the tape deck on. We did some crazy things; I was a horny little girl. But I wouldn't let him fuck me, not even with a rubber. He begged me and even went to the town library and got books that he made me read to see that there were times of the month when there was practically no chance. I still wouldn't. There was just too much to lose, wasn't there?

In the middle of the season my senior year, Randy Cobb took a job at the mill, second shift. He would lay out or get off early for my games. He had some money for the first time and spent it on me—some earrings I didn't like and a sweater

I did—when he didn't put it into the car. I got so I liked seeing him in the bleachers and would look for him during warm-ups or time-outs. One night when I was still working on my thousand points, I couldn't find him and played like hell the first half until Poppa Bear took me out and jerked me into line. Then he took me out again with about a minute to go in the game. We were ahead by ten, but still. I was expecting to get chewed out again, but instead he said, making me sit down beside him like he always did, "See that man," pointing across the way with his short fat finger to a fox-faced man in a black suit. I nodded. "He's the coach from Pfeiffer College and he wants to talk to you after the game. Think about what you're going to say." Pfeiffer College and Elon, those were it back before the ACC or any of the others had even thought about girls' basketball. We all knew about Pfeiffer. When he met me in the middle of the court after the game and told me I had played well and he was impressed and had had his eye on me for a long time, I was still looking around for Randy. When he said he would like me to play for him, I told him, "I don't think I want to go to college." He said he was sorry to hear it and that Coach had led him to believe otherwise, and wouldn't I give him a call if I changed my mind. Then he was gone, and after the boys' game I walked out to Snow's and called Randy.

I got my thousand points, but the season was a disappointment to Poppa Bear and me, too, because we lost in the state tournament. It was the first time we had ever lost the last game for him—state champs since I was in the tenth grade, and none of us knew how to take it. It was a team from Buncombe County we had never heard of, who had never come to state before. To see them you'd have to wonder how they ever got out of their conference, mousy and weak looking. But it was their coach. He was some kind of basketball genius and had cooked up four or five different full court presses, so every time we took the ball out, we were looking at something totally different. Whenever we went to pass the ball, it would be to one of them, not us. By halftime we were so mad we could have hit those girls, making us look like monkeys the way they did.

I should say that the whole secret of Poppa Bear's success as a coach is his halftime talk. At practice, he is all firm and fatherly when he's waddling around the floor showing you where to set up and how to get open and where the passes should go. He even laughs when one of the sophomores screws up and lands on her tail. At the games, though, it's hellfire. You can see it if you watch him on the bench, his face all red and snarly, his shirt all soaking wet. But buddy, that's nothing to what we got in his classroom where we'd go between halves. Sometimes he would just yell or throw a piece of chalk or an eraser. Others, he'd kick over the trash can and smash it in, rake the whole mess of books and papers right off his desk top, throw the books against the wall. And once, when it meant the regular season title, he took off the watch with the engraved back we'd given him the season before and stomped it until the little wheels and gears came out all over the floor. People used to wonder why, when the other team came back out on the run and went into their warm-ups, we walked out looking like we had just seen a car wreck. Well.

Now he came in and yelled around the Catawba College locker room where this tournament was, slammed some lockers and broke the clipboard he carried over his thigh. Even we could tell he was mostly acting this time and knew that we didn't need hellraising but some explaining. There was something that during the game Poppa Bear couldn't do. He'd never had to, not with us anyway. Afterwards he came in looking white and empty and patted each one of us on the head and hugged us which he'd never done, put his hands on us, even when we'd won the big games. Then he said, "I let you down, little women," and went out so we could shower. I pulled off my jersey and cried into it until my ribs hurt.

The week after graduation, a bunch of us girls went to Myrtle Beach for a week. Naturally, Randy and his friends went down, too, in his car. We had been diddling since the season was over, and it was nothing special. I was thinking about breaking up with him since he hadn't even graduated. Not because he was so dumb, because his mill job caused him to miss a lot. His other teachers understood and let him through with D's. Our English teacher wouldn't. So he was one credit short and never made it up.

Something happened down at the beach, though. I don't know whether it was the heat or the ocean or what, but it seems like Randy and I spent that whole week locking my friends or his out of the room and getting out of and then back into our clothes. I started to think maybe there was something more to Randy Cobb.

Then Monday after we got back, Mother pulled the rug right out from under me. I was sitting there flipping through *Vogue*, which she still gets though there's nothing in there she could wear, when she says, "You've got another thing coming if you think you're going to sit around here like the Queen of Sheba." So in two weeks I had a job in the piece goods department of Rose's where I still am today. It doesn't pay as much as the mill, but at least it's clean and quiet. I saved up, and Daddy helped me get a red doodle bug for close to cost. And Randy and I kept going out, driving out to the lake and screwing when it was a safe time for me, since we were both still living at home, and the rest of the time going to Charlotte and walking around the malls or going to some Burt Reynolds movie.

Poppa Bear called me up the weekend before Thanksgiving. It wasn't until then I realized I missed it, especially the practices. "Hey, old timer," he said, "how about getting some of you all together and coming over here to scrimmage with these little girls. They aren't going to do a thing without some competition." I was surprised how it came back to me. Without having touched a ball in months, I stepped on the court and made my first five shots. All day I was driving and shooting and passing like a wild woman. Maybe I was better than I ever was just by getting older. Afterwards, I thought of the black back of the Pfeiffer coach as he went out the double doors under the scoreboard and wondered if it was too late. But I went home and Randy came over, and we ate turkey with my folks and watched a football game on TV, and I forgot about it.

Poppa Bear would call me now and then for a few years, and I would go and have a good time. And I went to games some, too, just to hear the people tell me that I was better than anybody out there. Now Poppa Bear calls somebody younger I guess, but he still comes over to say hello to me in piece goods whenever he's in the store.

The next summer after I graduated, Randy said he wished I'd go on the pill. It made sense, all the worrying about my period being late and not wanting to get pregnant at all. So I went to Dr. Tynnes who had been my doctor since I was a girl. The way he looked at me made me think he was going to pick up the phone and call my mother, but he wrote the prescription. When I walked out of there, I felt like the whole waiting room knew and was staring right at me, and the way the nurses are at Dr. Tynnes', maybe they did. I was so mad I went out to the car and told Randy, "Damn, I'm so sick of this town. Let's go on and get married."

"Are you serious?" he said, looking me over. Then when he decided I was, he let out a big "Yahoo," and laid rubber all the way to the corner. Honestly and truly, I never understood what he was so excited about.

What's new then? Mother comes in Rose's and tells me there's a sale on all costume jewelry at Nelson's. What do I need with costume jewelry or lingerie or any of the other crap that Mother is always running down to Charlotte to buy? "You're letting yourself go," she tells me, meaning the weight on my thighs and arms and rear. But if I am, what about Randy whose big beer belly hangs out from under the black motorcycle T-shirts he wears around all the time? Is he the one I am supposed to be keeping myself up for? I would like to ask her this: Is it this bad with Daddy, was it this bad with Daddy after just five years, which is hard to believe? Does she feel as empty and lonely as I do sitting at home with the TV while Randy is off at the Rec Hall? But when I have tried to ask her—and I really haven't been a pest to her; I figured out money and sex without her help—she has cut me off. "Oh

7

honey," she says, and I can tell from her voice that her throat is full of cigarette smoke ready to boil out her mouth and nose, "If you'd asked me a long time ago I could have told you." Now I guess she thinks I can tough it out like she has. "I would never want *my* name to be Cobb," she always tells me as if that should have been reason enough.

Or she calls me on the phone to say that certain people have seen Randy at the What-a-Burger with some girl who wasn't me. Of course, it wasn't me since I am on the phone and Randy is gone in the car. My car, since he sold his old Ford a long time ago and bought a Honda 750 and matching helmets. He still owes on it. And I said then, "What are you going to pay for it with?" since he has been fired or quit at Burlington, Draymore, and Templon just since we've been married and now runs with a pack that call themselves painters. What am I supposed to do? Take his motorcycle and ride all over town to ask him what he wants from Mill Hill trash that he can't get from me? "Live and learn," Mother says, and the way she says it makes me think she is smiling.

This is why I am up in the bleachers watching Poppa Bear's girls finish practice. I want to ask him. It won't be long now; the star drill is always near the end. Poppa Bear says if you can make them when you're tired, you can make them anytime. So first there is running, then the star drill, then running, then free throws. At the end he calls his girls all into a circle in the center of the court where he praises the ones who deserve it and chews out the rest. Then he tells them about the next team and what to look for, what to think about. It is all strategy talk now—the blood doesn't flow until before the game. The girls make a cheer designed to jinx the other team and run off to their showers.

Poppa Bear walks off to the light switches at the far wall of the gym; I watch him in his small old man's waddle. He has the same old black framed glasses and his hair cut short, barely long enough to comb to one side in the front. He's so fat that he's nearly round, a fifty waist I'd guess; and he's the type who wears his pants up there around his chest. With a white towel crammed in his back pocket, he looks like an old draft horse, a nag. We laughed at him behind his back. All his girls have, I'm sure. But we knew he wanted us to win, to be something special, so when the time came, we obeyed him.

I go down to meet him as he comes down the dark floor. He is shorter than me, but I have never thought much of it before, thinking of him red faced and yelling—it stays with you. "You should come and show these girls how to shoot. You were the best shooter I ever had."

I smile at him, and we go into the coaches' office—always off limits to girls—where poster calendars from Carolina, State and Duke as well as girlie ones from parts and places here in town are all over the walls. There are broken down armchairs and trash cans crusty with tobacco juice. None of this mess is Poppa Bear's, who sits on the very edge of one of the ratty chairs and takes off his tiny black coaching shoes, the same pair I guess he's always had. His feet smell terrible, but I don't think he notices as he pulls off his white socks, stuffs them in his shoes and begins puttering around, washing his face and wiping it on his towel.

"Poppa Bear, do you remember Randy Cobb?"

"You were the best shooter I ever had," and I think he has forgotten he just told me that. But he says, "Maybe because when you were here we took extra practice every day while I was hoping he would go the hell away. Then I would see you in the phone booth by Snow's when I went home, calling him."

"Well, you were right," I tell him, but it doesn't make him glad. And I tell him all the rest as the girls go by the cracked open door and tell him good night as he stares at me. By now he has put on his street shoes and gotten his books and papers together. What does he do now? I have never thought; I don't even know where he lives. He fidgets and waits for me to finish.

He gets up and pats me on the shoulder, "Time to close the building." He's tired and I wonder why I came to him. There's not a blessed thing he could do about it. I go stand by the outside door and wait while he checks the windows and the locker room lights. Then as he lets us out the door, he

9

says, "I could have helped you once." We both know what he means.

Outside is my doodle bug ruined now from Randy's trying to make a dune buggy out of it by cutting the fenders funny with a blow torch and messing up the trunk and putting on funny tires and loud mufflers. It makes me sick. I get in and when I start it, it shakes all over; Randy's some mechanic. Maybe he will come in and expect his dinner; maybe I should hurry.

When I am driving and can't do anything else, I often think about my best games. I think now of the conference championship against Davie County, those ugly girls in their black sleeveless jerseys, looking like something off Roller Derby. They played us close the first half, but, of course, Poppa Bear put the fire in us at halftime. The next quarter, I hit seven shots in a row from the wing, which is where I was best from. Don't get me wrong, I could drive from out there too, left-handed even. But since they wanted to zone us, Annie, our point guard, would just come down the floor and drive into the zone, then dish to me where I'd be all alone out there and would pop it without even putting the ball on the floor. The last time, the goonie with her pigtails and braces had tears in her eyes when she came out to try to get a hand in my face.

Their coach called time out and put them in man-to-man, but they were broken, and we ran right through them. There was lots of fast breaking; once Poppa Bear got us started, he couldn't turn us except by taking the whole first team out. He didn't because he hated Davie as much as we did. Afterwards, I sat in the shower letting the hot water pour over me, smiling like a moron.

But now I guess I better hurry and pay attention to my driving. Randy will be home soon and want his dinner. I guess I could cut through the Mill Hill and then down onto Magnolia and up across Main Street to home. I pass the Baptist church. And there at the goal in the parking lot is a skinny little girl trying with all her might to get the ball up to the basket. Smart-mouthed boys on their knobby tire bikes ride by and tease her. Little girl, I'm thinking, I wish there was something I could tell you.

Monkeys

It was Spring Frolics in 1970, and we had all gone up the road to get drunk and throw bottles at the train. Up the road was Maggie's, just across the county line and the first place you came to that sold beer. It was just a cinderblock joint with a bar and some tables and booths. You could get food, too—there was a Coca-Cola menu offering hamburgers, cheeseburgers and a couple kinds of Stewart Sandwiches, gone yellow from grease over the grill—I made that mistake once. About the only thing that made Maggie's unique was a mural along one wall after Rousseau, a long way after him, I guess, of a bunch of monkeys sitting on the ground and in skinny trees. We all believed, and she never denied it, that Maggie herself had painted the mural. You could ask her why she did it, and if she was in a good mood and if she liked you, she might say something like, "It kind of reminds me of you boys, I guess." We liked that and cut our initials or those of our frats into the monkeys' bodies. There were coconuts too, I remember.

Maggie's was then the biggest Bud distributor in North Carolina. We gave her that distinction, and so we felt like we had the right to get together one Thursday night a year and piss in the road and set the big trash barrels on fire and stop traffic. And when the pitiful six-car freight made its way from Charlotte up to Mooresville to take on a few more boxes from the textile mills and then go on until it finally got to Greensboro or wherever and began to look like a respectable train, we ran across the highway to meet it with every empty bottle we had managed to put by. It occurs to me that there was more to Maggie's saying we reminded her of monkeys than any of us would have given her credit for at the time.

Maggie would wait until we had piled in our cars. They were nice cars, new cars—ours was a rich school for gentlemen from better families—and gotten a good start down the road before she called the cops. And I guess they took their time showing up, too. Nobody knew what the Southern Railroad thought of it.

Because I wanted to have lots of bottles, I'd gotten there early. And when the bad business I am about to tell you about happened, I would say I had eight or nine bottles in front of me. I was calling them "my babies," and I was leaning on the table with my arm around them just in case somebody came by and tried to sneak one away when I wasn't looking. I was feeling pretty happy.

I always liked to sit under the monkey with two coconuts held against his stomach, looking down like he could drop them on top of you if you caused him any trouble. Except somebody had gotten in there and drawn on them until, in the right light, you could see the pencil lines that made them two enormous tits. Drawn in over those were other lines making vanes stuck on the tails of bombs.

"This is some kind of symbol," I said to the guy across the table. I knew him, we lived on the same hall and had bummed a ride up together. Anybody would give you a ride to Maggie's. "These could be what? Little Boy and Fat Man? Look at that monkey and tell me if you don't see a little God-fucking-Oppy-Oppenheimer in him. It's his grin." This guy, Mike, was sober. He'd had a beer and taken the bottle back to the bar and now he was drinking an orange soda. He pissed me off, and I thought I had a right to be. I'd asked for that beer bottle since I knew he wasn't going to use it, and he'd said no. I was even more pissed because Maggie took it. It's funny because she didn't exactly want us to bust up the bottles on the train; they were long-necks, returnables, but she was resigned. But for Mike to give one back made him just as much of a little shit in her eyes as in mine. This may be how you have to think if you are going to run a beer joint, I don't know.

"Or," I said, "these are Earth Mammas One and Two, chocolate and vanilla, giving suck to the world." I put my hand up to the coconuts and pushed my fingertips against the wall, cool and sweating. I remember that. And I was thinking what would it take to will them to three-dimensionality, to feel the soft weight of flesh in my palms? "Huma, huma, just like Miss July, the one with the jugs so big and sitting in that little swinging basket. You know." I looked at him, and like some kind of tar baby he just sat there. He knew. We had been freshman together when Sanders took a whole stack of those magazines and cut them up and made a whole wall of nothing but tits. We thought that was heaven, just sitting around the room looking at a *Playboy* with no mom nowhere to catch you at it. We'd never admit it, never admit we all hung back one time or another when everybody was heading to supper and beat off in our rooms. There was lots of wild talk until we ended up going down to Charlotte and prowling around Queens College all weekend just looking for girls. We saw some, they saw us.

And somehow everybody all got together. It was that kind of fucking you do when you're young, something mean behind it, both of you do it again and again and all for yourself. Except the one I hooked up with from UNC-C. It was hard for her; she hated my friends. And maybe she was right. They were the rich ones with the nice cars I was talking about, and I guess I wasn't. I wasn't poor and never felt poor until I went to school there. And it was the same for her. The girls from Queens were just like the guys I knew. And they were all good at sizing each other up. For the guys it was a bathroom wall kind of equation worked out in tits and asses and legs. And for the girls it had more to do with the labels you had inside your clothes. You could call them bastards and bitches, but it was just the way they had been brought up thinking it was OK to want lots of everything. So getting laid and getting drunk, they were able to take what might look like greed and make it pass for love.

Mine and I broke up. She was Mickey, nobody from Queens was a Mickey. And she was a sweet woman and kind and tried to love me, honest to Christ. I think I could have loved her if she had been able to get ahold of me right out of high school. Her kind of sweet loving, that kind that makes you buy ceramic what-nots with the other party's name on them and not be ashamed, is what I always wish I could get back to. Even then it was late, and now it is too late. You could call it the price you pay. That would be fair, but I didn't know.

She dropped me about two weeks before the train came. It was a question of style. When we went into a room at a frat party you could see it, the difference between clothes that come from Belk's and not one of the stores that has a name like Town'N'Tweed and never has to advertise. My clothes were from Belk's, too, but on me nobody had minded. People knew me and besides I played football. Up to a point, I was OK.

For Mickey, it was maybe too easy to see where the point was located, but I wasn't ready to admit it. There were some things I could have learned about myself a lot easier if I had listened to Mickey, stayed sober and not gone up the road so much. But I wasn't interested in knowing anything yet.

I told Mike he was a pussy, which was something we said to each other from time to time just to show affection. But this time I said it a little different, so Mike pulled his head back; he knew it had been an insult. He looked like a damn junior high kid with his contacts out and these Buddy Holly glasses he had on, and I told him that, too. "What crawled up your ass?" he said. He gave his beer bottle back to Maggie, that was what. And now he was going to take that pop bottle back up there, too. Hell, I wasn't even sure that you could throw a pop bottle at the train; or it might not have been the right thing to do, but it was a bottle and because of Mickey I thought I had some right to be a bastard.

15

You end up knowing a lot about a guy when you live around him. There is no real privacy in a dorm, sooner or later everybody gets caught dating Rosie Palm, and it just becomes something you know about each other. Back in the fall, Mike and I had sat in the lobby on our floor like everybody else watching them draw the numbers for the draft lottery. Most of us had gone off to Maggie's after that, too, but in lots of different moods. I got drunk that night, saying as I did that it would take the return of Fat Man himself to get my ass drafted, my number was 325, and by then there wouldn't be a me or anybody left to draft me. I was in ROTC and like half the campus, I turned in my junk the next day, just walked, took my F without even finishing the term out.

Mike didn't go up the road with us, and we talked about him sticking back at the dorm pulling his sober-sided shit. His number was high, the middle 200's, I think, and he was from Raleigh. He was home clear, too. But we were there, maybe right in the same very booth with Oppy-Mamma Suck, four of us big winners wondering about Mike. He had been angling for a CO and now that he had his number, you would have thought he would just drop it. But I heard later he would go on through with it. To quit now would just prove he was only doing it to save his ass. I'd assumed he was doing it to save his ass; I thought anybody would do it to save his ass. The difference between Mike and me, I said, was that if I would have walked into a room of old farts and told them I was a pacifist, they would have laughed in my face.

I guess they would have been right. Because I was hugging my empties and looking at Mike, whose eyes always looked red-rimmed behind his glasses. I was focusing on his two Bic Accountant fine-point pens and his little black appointment book stuffed in his shirt pocket. I was picturing his white basketball shoes down under the table when he never played ball. I was looking at Mike and deciding to hate him.

This was a trick an old high school line coach taught me, a man that I once believed was the dumbest man alive. But now I know he was smart, smart in the way a big rock or a tree is smart, smarter than you are just because it's been around so long and intends to stay even longer. Maybe you will be around in the morning and maybe you won't. And even though that bastard got fired from the school I went to, I know he is out there coaching somewhere. He would have a way of making himself useful.

He taught me meanness. He could teach it to anybody, even Buddy Burke who was a sophomore when I finished and who went on to be an all-state tackle and go to Clemson and started out as the sweetest boy I ever saw. Two hundred pounds, and he would let some skinny-assed wideout smack him on the head. But that coach was on Buddy's case twenty-four hours a day, even in the lunch room making fun of what he ate. Even in the shower making fun of his dick. And by his junior and senior years, Buddy Burke was so full of hate that other teams and his teachers and even the town cops were scared to come close to him.

This coach would say to us before the game to look at the man you played head up on the other side of the line and find something about him that made you sick. It could be a pimple on his neck where his pads rubbed, it could be his puny attempt to grow a moustache. Look at that until it made you so sick you hated that guy. This worked for me, but I think most of the guys I played with just thought of coach.

"Mike," I said, "are you afraid that if you throw a bottle at the train somebody will tell the draft board?"

"Fuck you," he said and moved his soda bottle to his side of the table to protect it. "Just because Mickey dumped on you doesn't give you the right to be a bastard."

"I guess it does," I told him. And I realized that I meant it. It was funny, I was drunk enough to hover out over my body and see myself acting this way and just let whatever was going to happen go on and happen.

This was a new sensation for me. In football it's just the opposite—your consciousness is nowhere. You go for sixty minutes and you never really think about anything at all. Sure you run all over the field giving and getting all sorts of shit and run off and coach sticks a pint-sized chalkboard in your face and hollers amazing things about seams and zones and keying off. And you sort of grunt. You go a whole afternoon and never say a sentence.

How, Mickey wanted to know, could I keep playing when somebody I had just knocked the piss out of was lying face down not moving five yards away? And that is the answer, my mind just wasn't there. To go over and look at the guy, to say you're sorry would take you into another way of thinking. And it's not that you don't want to go up, it's that it just never occurs to you to do it. A trainer comes running out to stick an am-cap under the zonked guy's nose, and the whole team stands around idling like a Peterbilt at a truck stop.

What was going on between Mike and me was another thing entirely. I wanted to fight Mike although football is supposed to make people channel their meanness. Who could believe that if they had seen Buddy Burke and knew what happened to him (which was that he discharged a twelve-gauge shotgun into another jock's door for playing his radio on the wrong station and put about two dozen pellets in that boy's chest and proved himself too mean for Clemson even)? And what was I trying to prove to Mike anyhow?

I wasn't sure except what I was saying was that nobody but a fool could be a CO, that we were all a bunch of gorillas busting each other's nuts and a CO was the monkey who just covered his eyes. There were no innocent looking monkeys in Maggie's mural, all were looking out into that beer joint taking it all in.

Mike was saying something altogether different to me, too. He was trying to talk to me about Mickey. I was drunk enough so everything he said was going into my brain on a delayed basis, sort of like the calls on a phone-in talk show. What I was hearing and actually taking in, though I don't think I ever said anything to Mike that would give him a clue, was that even though I had been a bastard to Mickey and everybody knew it, they thought they could forgive me. I had been going through a lot, too, what with having a bad GPA and not starting on the football team.

18

As I said, when you live on the same hall with people, things get around. Sure, Mickey and I had these hellacious fights; they were maybe more entertaining than our sex which everybody was tuned in on, too. We didn't hit each other, but I know I cocked my arm back a time or two. Before she met me, I doubt if she would have ever thought such awful words were possible. Because all these fights, and I can't remember what any of them were actually about, always ended the same way: Mickey would start bawling. She would flop face down on my bed and would sound like she was going to hyperventilate right there. We always managed to get into these fights half-naked so there would be the extra visual slap of her bare back quivering with goose bumps. It amazed me that I could make somebody cry, and it made me feel strong.

If I had been into thinking in those days, those fights with Mickey would have given me a lot to think about. If I had been thinking the Spring Frolic night I had it out with Mike, maybe I could have saved myself some grief. Because I knew as we sat there, me yelling and him into some counselor mode that he must have picked up in a psych. course, that I was never going to play a game of football again. That I was going to leave this gentleman's college and find one that was more for people like me. I could say I knew these things, but if I did I had yet to talk to myself about them.

People who saw me play in high school would tell you I was a hell of a football player. And they would wonder why I never did anything in college. I could tell them now. Before a football game you are liable to see players doing crazy stuff to themselves, to each other. Mickey used to ask me about this, how I did it, what it felt like, because I would go up to a guy and just bash on his shoulder pads with my bare forearms, then we would smack each other on the helmet, throw shivers into each other's guts. My answer would be that I never felt a thing. This is why I played. And in high school that had always been enough. I didn't necessarily want to inflict pain, but it was the nature of the game. I should say I was never hurt bad; I had my clock cleaned but never landed in the hospital.

19

So for me it was just a hundred-yard party. If I took a fake, even if I got blocked down, I could get up and get back into it. I was just a fast kid who loved running into people.

In college, they expect you to think, to make little maps in your mind of coverages and areas of responsibility. You could knock a guy on his ass, and it would just come out a mistake. That wasn't why I played the game. Their way only spoiled it.

I had just about decided that the whole reason Mike was on me so bad about Mickey was that he had the hots for her. That he was thinking that he could jump in there and save her battered psyche. So Mike's voice coming in and my own hollering about CO's being pussies now fell into congruent patterns. "Mike," I told him, "you can have Mickey; she'd be a good match with you, she isn't into fighting, either. But I would have to beat your ass to make it all even. Do you see how that would work?" He looked at me, and I could tell he was trying to separate the drunk talk from the talk talk, which was more than I could do. Mike didn't know that, though.

The place was emptying out. It was 11:20 by the Dr. Pepper clock known to be ten minutes slow to accomodate last-minute beer runs, and the train was due at 11:25 real time, so everybody was trying to be sneaky in not so sneaky ways while carrying their bottles out into the parking lot. "We should talk about this tomorrow, when you're in a better mood," Mike told me. And I said, "Mike, are you going to use that bottle on the train?" "No," he told me and started for the bar with it.

Except that I tackled him before he got there, and the bottle went rolling off in one direction, and Mike's glasses went in another and he spilled his pens and little black book. And I helped him up and then hit him in the face as hard as I could. There were still some guys in there, and I guess they had been trying to decide whether we were joking or not. Now that they knew, they were too worried about Mike and probably too scared to mess with me.

I went on out empty handed and started down the road. People were yelling at me to come back, saying I couldn't leave now, and finally asking if they could have my bottles. I didn't even wave, I cut off the road as soon as I got into the dark, taking the woods until they opened onto the cross-country trail. I took that to where it ran behind the baseball field. That was as far as I could make it; I climbed the fence and crawled into the dugout to sleep it off.

That was the Spring Frolics the train never came. Nobody knows why. Everybody said it was because some rat had called the Southern Railroad office in Charlotte and tipped them off. But it could have been that there just wasn't enough freight to make up a train. So my run-in with Mike had been the event of the evening that everybody was talking about. He was over in the infirmary with a broken jaw and six stitches in the back of his head. I couldn't know that as I sat in the dugout and put off walking up the hill to the dorms as long as I could. A lot of decisions had been made for me, but I didn't know that either.

I think about Mike often enough, though the last anybody ever wrote me was about his CO going through. He's probably in Appalachia teaching hillbilly kids how to read or helping some African tribe dig a well and drive their tractor. He would be that kind of guy. And I guess I tell this story because I am ashamed of what I did that night. But I can't really say I'm sorry.

Jackson Of All Trades

Another thing about his ex-girlfriend was she never let him stay to the end of movies. As soon as the last scene was over, she would be headed up the aisle, dragging Jackson by the crook of his arm like a trouble-making kid. He'd be walking backwards, still watching the credits rolling, the theme song winding it all up. He was happy with that compromise until they got to the top, then it would be, "Wait, just wait a minute," digging his heels into the carpet until the little globe came up onto the screen and stopped, signaling the true end. At first she thought it was funny. "Do you really care who the make-up artist is? Do you even know what a key grip does?" Of course he didn't; that was beside the point, the point being to see it through. That's why you might see him sitting in the stands of rainy forty-to-nothing ball games, at rock concerts after the last match for encore has gone out and the roadies are looping up the microphone wires. She laughed. He said, "You've got to understand that's the way I am. I like things to come out even, to be complete and done." After a while she stopped thinking it was funny.

Her name was Denny, short for Denise, and she stuck him with a house to get rid of. Now she calls him on the WATS line from her new job in D. C. and tells him, "Sell it for God's sake. You can't keep up the payments on what you make." She's right, of course, but Jackson tells her to fuck off and hangs up on her. He tells her to fuck off often. It doesn't do any good; he still loves her.

If you'd known them then, you would have thought it was nothing special. But to Jackson the vibes were inescapable. For example, they were both math majors in college. And the way they met, their bumpers locking when she drifted her car back into his truck at the stoplight out by Hill's. Denny was drunk, but Jackson got the cars loose by bouncing on her bumper before any cops showed up. Taking advantage of his corny luck, he offered to buy her another drink now that they were acquainted. "Thanks, but I think I've already had enough," she'd said, Jackson finishing the sentence with her. After that they finished lots of sentences together. "See what I mean?" Jackson will tell you, "inescapable." Except now she claims he did it on purpose.

That doesn't account for the garden either, does it? The garden that had been kept on the plot behind their house for over a hundred straight years. They learned about it from the old neighbor lady who talked to them all the time until she found out they weren't married, just living together. But Denny had already been out there looking over the plot and down to the library for a couple of dozen books on how it was done. You'll see that's how Denny was, diving headfirst into things she didn't know anything about. The garden worked. She read around in her books until she settled on this French way of making little individual built-up plots for each crop, probably because nobody in Radford ever did anything like it. Now I hear all the hippies down in Floyd County say it's the only way to go. She was like that, put her in a New York ad agency, and she could make you a million in a week.

She also got tired of that garden about three weeks after the first sprouts came up. Jackson put out the pie tins to keep the birds off, sat up at night to shoot the ground hog even though it wasn't in his nature to do it. He's getting ripe tomatoes at about a dozen a day, green peppers, little but perfectly shaped, squash, zucchini, sweet corn. Now that they're back on speaking terms, it's all she can talk about, how well it

23

turned out, how Jackson must have a green thumb and won't he tell her his secret? She, the neighbor lady, not she, Denny.

She, Denny, never stopped talking to him. She talked to Jackson like somebody she'd lived in the same dorm with, shared a couple of classes together, had lunch with a time or two. Casual and interested, concerned even if she ever saw you with your arm in a sling. "Christ," Jackson tells her, "You're twisting my nuts off."

She sighs, "Don't be so melodramatic."

"OK. What do you want me to do with the quilting frame?"

"Sell it? Give it away? You decide, you made it."

It wasn't too hard. Jackson's a clever guy, good with his hands. No finished carpentry, but he can build you a sun deck like everybody's got to have these days. Can do a little mechanicing, paint your house, bartend, lifeguard. That's how he makes it, how he made it before Denny.

You might say he's the glue that holds a place like Radford together. When you need some cord wood, who do you call? Come and fix the washer? He'll try it, do the job right or make it right. And his prices are good, especially if it's cash or swap (no taxes, see). After a while, people get to know you if you do good work. They remember. And Jackson's been here eight years. He's not hard to find. Call him at home or look for his pick up on Norwood. Anybody can point it out.

Denny never could accept the way Jackson made his living. Not that the money was bad; it was just too irregular. What did he put in the income tax blank under occupation, handyman? As to the math major biz, she couldn't understand why he wasn't using his degree. "I never thought linear algebra was a philosophy to live by." Which wasn't what she meant, of course, since she worked in the computer center over at Virginia Tech. But was she any happier for sitting all day in front of a video display unit? She wouldn't answer him that.

She went to his old place once, the old garage apartment, along with half the garage under it for his tools and stuff he rented from a professor. It was a good set-up. Jackson put up the drywall, put in the plumbing himself. He laid it out like a loft, the efficiency kitchen backed up against the bathroom to save on the pipe. Except for the fifty-watt system and the records and tapes that went with it, you might think a monk lived there. He had his small collection of books, mostly sci-fi left over from college, a solid oak work table. After that, nothing but a couple of stuffing-busted armchairs, a card table and chairs. The clean and pleasing smell of WD-40 permeated the place.

At the time, he was overhauling a chainsaw that some bozo had ruined by leaving gas in it all spring and summer. It's the kind of job Jackson gets, one too embarrassing to take back to the store for servicing. Now the saw was all apart, cleaned and spread out over old newspapers just waiting for the parts to come for reassembling. When he looked at it, he saw it with a trick-photographer's eye, imploding into its original perfect condition.

"How can you live like this?" Denny had asked, throwing her hands out at him like she was dumping a wheelbarrow load of shit into his lap. Jackson had smiled and shrugged. You might wonder why he didn't see then what it would come to, but he had already fallen in love.

Here's how it happened: After he got the cars loose, Jackson called Denny up and she said OK. Not much happened though, despite Jackson's telling her it was inevitable. "What do you think our cars were trying to tell us when they ran together?" She just arched her eyebrow. Still, when he asked her to go to the West Virginia State Fair after an uneventful night of pizza and beer, she accepted. Once you get away from the college dating circuit, there just aren't many chances, are there?

Jackson liked the fair and would have gone even if she hadn't taken him up on it. Since he was a kid, he'd gone back every year just to see the trotters run. She let him drive her car—she didn't trust his truck—and he drove well, carefully and fast. Denny liked that. She also liked the fair, more than Jackson did as it turned out. When they went through the livestock exhibitions, she surprised him by talking to the sheep and rabbits and massive draft horses. Then she had to go through the halls with the 4-H displays on safety in the home, and mental health, and the basic food groups. And the canned stuff, the baked goods and crafts. Jackson could hear the announcer calling the races. As long as Denny was having a good time, he tried not to show his impatience. Up to then it had been a job for him to keep thinking up what they would do next. Always when he left her apartment after a date, he sat in the truck for a minute or so before starting the engine wondering what the hell.

They went out on the midway and made the circuit of rides designed for teenagers in love, the double ferris wheel, the Octopus where you can't help getting slammed into each other, the dumb toboggan thing with the DJ type operator who plays pop music and patters while you just go round and round and neck. Jackson even tried to win her a stuffed animal. When a scalper offered him a really good price on a pair of tickets to Crystal Gayle and Denny even liked that, Jackson got to thinking that back in Radford he might get asked to spend the night.

It didn't happen, and he'd just about decided to forget it, not even call her again, when Denny called him the very next day. He went over. She met him at the door, having done herself up with some kind of new make-up around the eyes, tending toward the pink and beige, wearing a plaid shirt with a thread of gold worked through it, unbuttoned down to the tops of her breasts, jeans, and sandals. Cowgirl: Jackson got the connection. And in the kitchen, he watched the finishing touches go on a rhubarb and strawberry pie with lattice crust before it went in the oven.

Afterwards on the balcony, with the pie and coffee, she asked him, "What do you want out of life anyway?"

He looked at her and smiled, said, "Something like this."

She went over and sat down against him on the sunning chair. "I was hoping you'd say that."

What, he would have liked to ask her, do you want? But there was something in the warmth and moisture of her

26

kisses that hadn't quite been there before, so he never got around to it.

Nobody saw much of him for several weeks after that. Call him at home, no answer. Look for him where you might usually find him, Carol Lee for breakfast, Missile Command in the evenings at Silver Odyssey, maybe the outdoor hoops behind the Radford gym. You could catch him at Paul's, the bike store, where he put in a night's mechanicing every Monday. Where's he been? He'd just smile. Sly dog, but it was hard not to be happy for him.

This was when he built the quilting frame. Denny decided to take up the life represented by the West Virginia State Fair. As for the quilting, it seemed as good a place as any to start. She went to the library and got a stack of books and started a six-point star pattern, which was a harder trick to pull off than the garden was later since Denny couldn't even sew on a machine, much less by hand. Give her credit, though, she stuck with it all winter, made the whole top of the quilt and started it onto the backing after they moved in the house in the spring.

It seemed perfect for them, lots of work but the potential was there. Jackson went right to it, refinishing the floors, new wallpaper, a big Fisher woodstove in what they were calling the workroom, where the quilt sat on its frame, still sits with the backing halfway on. And convenient, the house being on Grove, the old Radford College faculty row, so Jackson's friends started thinking of it as their clubhouse. For a while, Denny liked them, liked getting to play the mother sitting in the middle of them in her big rocker braiding on a rug. They're all right, the kind of guys who live for summer softball leagues, or playing guitar in a band, or painting pictures that never seem to get started, and pick their jobs accordingly. As long as there's some gas in the car, good dope and the rent's paid, isn't that about enough? Some of them have women, hairy-legged things who stay home in the old shacks and trailers down around the river. How could they live like that, Denny wondered, when she saw how the husbands were, leaving their empties full of ashes all over the house. Then she broke down and threw them all out.

Jackson didn't seem to mind. He had never lived with a woman before, and every day he fell more in love with Denny, him still half asleep and naked in the bed watching her put on her good clothes to go to work. Watching her in the afternoons as she pulled them off, wanting her every time he saw her in her stockings and her slip. When he tried to tug her onto the bed, she'd usually resist him. Even in that he loved her more. Maybe she was already drifting away. But for Jackson, things had never been more complete despite his never thinking of himself as incomplete before.

You can't blame her much. Anybody who can change her life based on a one-day visit to the fair is just as likely to change it back. To Jackson's mind, it all turned around the bedroom. There he did his best work, the stuccoed ceiling, the white cured plaster walls, except the back wall of wide white oak slabs, grooved and joined coming down the wall in chevrons. All the woodwork was natural oak. The iron bedstead he'd sandblasted to the metal and refinished in an almost liquid indigo stood in the center away from the wall, bare except for framed illustrations, old *Vogue* covers. The arrangement was all Denny's idea, copied from a shoe advertisement. With the covers thrown back, Denny's gown which barely covered her ass thrown carelessly over the footboard, it was a beautiful room. Bed made, knowing the closet on her side was empty, it was cold. The heat never circulated up there anyway. Jackson took to sleeping on the floor in the work room.

There he was living in that house booby-trapped like a minefield with the stuff Denny had left behind by accident, stray underwear in the bottom of the basket, her rings on the shelf above the kitchen sink. Or on purpose, the crafts crap, of course, which didn't mesh at all with her new life at double the salary and doing the same thing she had been at Tech and now into the New Music scene in the Washington area. Look for her in the Nine-thirty Club if you're up that way. And Jackson wasn't talking to anybody except Paul.

Jackson and Paul go back a few years. It's a good arrangement for both of them. Paul's shop is strictly a one-man operation, he sells more used bikes than new, but he gets behind. So every Monday night, Jackson comes by and has a few beers and helps catch up on the repairs. They put Paul's portable TV on top of the mini fridge and watch Monday Night Football or Baseball depending on the season. And when there isn't any Monday night game, it's usually too deep in the winter to have many repairs.

Paul saves the complete overhauls, the wheel building, for Jackson who likes those jobs; and to tell you the truth, Jackson's the better mechanic, and Paul knows it. And he's fast. Maybe it's only because Paul's been there all day already, but he finds himself standing with wrench in his hand listening while Jackson, like a good barber, works as fast as he talks.

He takes up this job with pleasure, new wheels, four-crossed butted spokes on Weinmann alloy rims and Phil hubs, solid touring wheels for somebody who knows what he wants. Jackson takes Paul's crazy round slide rule down and figures the spoke length. "I just wish she would fight about it," he tells Paul.

"Fuck her. It's over."

"Oh hell, maybe so." Do you think this settles anything? Jackson sits on the camp stool and laces the wheel, takes the spoke wrench and tightens the nipples down to the thread tops, picks up the wheel and breaks it—bends over it and flexes it with his body and arms. Then he takes it up to the truing jig, the home-made jig he built for this shop, for Paul, and begins to true the wheel. This could take him hours, but Paul has set a limit of forty-five minutes per wheel. The Polish Olympic team, they say, rode on wheels trued for twenty-four hours. What difference could it make when one pothole might ruin it all? It matters to Jackson.

"You know what it's like. Just being around her, just in the kitchen getting together the salad stuff and being able to reach over and grab her ass."

"Forget it. She cleaned up your eating habits, that's about it."

"More," Jackson claims. And he works the wheel in the incremental adjustments of a quarter turn, an eighth turn on one spoke and then the opposite on its neighbor. Taking the wheel out, breaking it, starting again. Always tightening down the tolerance screws he works the wheel between.

They are making fun of Yogi Berra on the ball game, the last baseball of the year. They make fun of Yogi on a weekly basis, a running gag on this show. Jackson hates them for it, he remembers the Yog in uniform, a better player than any of them. "He was right," Jackson says, the almost heart-shaped spoke wrench hanging off his finger as he points at the screen, "It ain't over til it's over." He spins the wheel, watches its perfect track. This is what he wanted, isn't it?

Now it is late in the fall. Jackson sits on the back porch in his sweatshirt and looks at the garden. Even though the frost has not come, the garden is drying up. No more corn or peppers. The tomatoes are small and shriveled; they can't seem to get enough juice. This is the way she left him:

She got a U-Haul hitched to her Camaro and Jackson helped her load it out. "You don't even have a job there."

"I can get one." He'd seen the classifieds in the *Post*. She was right.

"What's wrong with this?"

"Nothing." Not a lie really. "It's just not me, is it?"

"But I love you."

"I never said that."

She hadn't. "Jesus, look at what those bastards at the gas station did to your bumper," he told her, disapproving of how they'd just clamped the tow hitch on without even trying to save the chrome.

"That's nothing, it doesn't matter."

As he stood in the street watching her pull out, he didn't understand he'd lost his chance to have his say.

When the old lady hangs her head over the fence and tells him she knew Denny was the type anyhow, she doesn't know how close she's coming. Jackson just grunts. He looks at the garage down at the end of the yard, leaning into a parallelogram. Denny had been after him to straighten it up, the only thing about the house he never got done. He tried to explain to her the wood was too old and brittle, not rotten. To try to straighten it with jacks would only split it up. Besides, he liked it crooked. It was for him, his tools and solvents, brushes and paint; the house was Denny's. Now he sees it different. Though it's too late in the day and won't be light much longer, he goes to the shed and cleans it out, takes up his wrecking bar and begins to prize off the sideboards slowly and carefully so they can be replaced. He'll right the thing, then get the hell out.

Three Weird Things

So he calls me up and says do I want to go fishing? When? I want to know. Leave Friday at lunch, he says like it's the easiest thing in the world if you're a legal secretary to just walk in your boss's office and tell him you're going fishing. Well, it so happens that Mr. Samples will be out Friday, but he, Erlichman, doesn't have to know that.

What kind of fishing? Trout fishing, he says and starts right in to all these lies about us staying in a lodge where they bring breakfast up to your room, and you can look out from this little balcony and see deers feeding in the meadow. And I start saying right over top him, and the bugs, and it'll probably rain, and the mud, and…. Do you want to go or not? he says. Let me think about it, I say. I look up at the TV and it's "The Waltons," ugh, and then I happen to think that Janie's (that's my roommate) Mom and Daddy are driving up from Spartanburg to see how their little girl is doing in the city. I swear they come every other weekend, it seems like, and it's like a Sunday School. Yeah, I tell him.

Erlichman. He's a butthole, if you know what I mean. I met him about six months ago when Janie first moved in with me (my other roommate got married), and I was showing her the town. I went in this place down on Independence where I don't usually go, Xanadu or something like that, where, besides a dance floor, they have all these pinball machines and other games. Erlichman's there, and Janie kind of likes him, but he likes me better I can tell. Janie's kind of heavy for one thing—she could do something about it if she'd try.

We all three play one of the machines—Future Spa with these space age joggers running up where the scores go and this one has electronic numbers instead of the old flip-up kind like used to be on the Jack of Diamonds machine in O. C.'s Shell station when I was a kid. Erlichman is real good at playing pinball, and Janie and me, of course, are just giggling and wasting our money. Every now and then I would feel bad because I could see that Erlichman would end up with me if I wanted him and because Janie was my new roommate and all. I didn't think it would be the first time somebody snaked her though.

Erlichman, though, I decided, why not? He was a mover, but he was different. For one thing he didn't have on the usual trashy clothes you see on guys around Charlotte, no nylon shirt unbuttoned halfway down and neck chains and jogging shoes. No, he looked like somebody that might have been in the firm (Samples and Leggat, where I work—for Mr. Samples Sr. personally). His hair was real short and dark, and he had on a navy blazer and good gray flannel slacks, no tie, but you could tell he probably left it in the car. So I thought maybe he's a stockbroker or an attorney.

I was wrong. Surprised? I get used to it. He's nothing but a small time Realtor—he won't tell me what kind of listings he's got. But he still looks like somebody who knows his way around ought to look. You never can tell, he might make a big sale, co-broke it with a hot shot or something (it happens) and then he would be set.

It's worth waiting around for a while. One thing's for sure, nothing's ever going to come my way down at the firm. The first couple of years I was there I would go out with the young ones right out of law school (I never went around with any of the married ones, at least not after I found out). I thought, you know, that they would get serious. I'm smart enough— I've been there five years and I can tell you that I know some tricks about the law that they don't know coming fresh out of law school. But it's because I'm a secretary that it was OK to take me out to dinner and the rest and then get married to some dumb girl with big framed glasses (I wear contacts myself) because she's got a college education and carries a book around in her purse.

Erlichman comes right in the middle of "The Young and the Restless" which I get to see hardly at all as it is because of work. But Erlichman being the way he is won't wait until it's over—only fifteen minutes. He takes one look at me and says, I hope those aren't the only shoes you're taking. What's wrong with these shoes I'd like to know, I tell him (they're sandals with wedge heels, not too high.) He tells me we're going to be walking up and down hills. I like that, the way he tells me this at the last minute. So I go back to my bedroom and look for some shoes to walk in. Erlichman can make me feel like such a twit. I want to go out there and tell him to stick his fishing pole up his ass and get on out of here. And I would, too, if Janie's parents weren't going to come, and I wouldn't even be able to have a beer all day Saturday much less mix up something in the blender. And then Sunday I would have to get up and go with them to a big old Baptist church up on Eastway, cold as a barn, where the preacher sounds like somebody getting up to read his quarterly report at a board meeting and no gospel choir. I don't care about church anyway, but you ought to have some spirit about it. I find some tennis shoes and squeeze them into my bag which ruins the way I packed it so neat last night, the way my roommate (not Janie, she's a teller in training with Wachovia Bank, the branch on Central. It's ruining her ankles) who was a stewardess and got married showed me in the kind of tear-shaped American Tourister bag that they all carry. Don't ever check your bag she told me, the ground people go through them. A bag like mine fits over your head on the plane—I take it whenever I go with Mr. Samples. I pick up my bag and sling it up on my shoulder and don't stop walking until I'm out the door and Erlichman is still sitting in the swivel lounge chair gawking after me. What are you waiting on? I say.

Outside Erlichman does what I consider to be his worst habit, he just looks around with his lip all curled up like if he was God he would wipe my complex off the face of the earth. I'll admit it's not so pretty outside. There are some broken down cars in the parking lot and everybody chains their motorcycles and canoes and stuff to the posts holding up the balcony. Still, everything is kept up inside. Erlichman doesn't think so, of course. Our apartment used to look nicer before my roommate moved out and took her travel posters down off the walls in the living room. But I have some things I'm proud of. I have a nice bed that used to belong to my grandmother. It's an iron bedstead and used to have springs and a feather mattress, but my daddy fixed it for me with two by fours so I could put a regular mattress and box springs on it. And there is an old rocker with a cane bottom that was Granny's. It has brown porch paint on it now, but I'm going to scrape it all off and fix it up one Saturday. And I have a cedar chest. That just goes to show you how times change. My mom bought that hope chest for me when I was in the eighth grade. I was supposed to learn how to sew in home ec. and make all kinds of things to go in it for you-know-when. I made a couple of squares on a quilt (log cabin pattern) and threw them in there, and that's as far as I got. But it's a good thing to have to store your winter clothes; they smell so nice when you get them out.

I expect Erlichman to say something like he usually does about the run down parking lot but I guess he's so happy that we're finally starting on his precious fishing trip that he forgets and goes straight to the car. He has his fishing gear all laid out in the trunk like he was posing it for a picture. Really, it reminds me of this picture that used to be over the doctor's desk in his office back in Harmony, N. C., where I went when I was little. There was a fancy expensive rod and a reel with holes drilled through it and a wicker creel just like Erlichman's (you could maybe make a pretty purse out of something like that if you lined it with some material—to carry on picnics and things like that), and these three dead fish staring out at you. You never went into the room with

35

the fish and sat right there beside the desk unless you were going to have your blood pressure taken or to get a shot. When you're a seven-year-old girl, you don't need your blood pressure taken too much, so when the doctor told me to go in and sit at the desk (he liked to pull the slide board that the typewriter's supposed to go on out to brace your arm, that's how come the desk) I always knew what was coming. The doctor would be back in the examination room humming his little song with no real tune to it while he was getting the needle out of the sterilizer, and I would sit there and look at the dead fish and say, boy, do I know how you feel.

I don't even think about putting my bag into the trunk until Erlichman has shifted his stuff around. I can tell it hurts him to break up his little arrangement. Where's my rod? I want to know. There's only one rod in there, I tell him. Oh yeah, he says, pretending like he just now thought of it. More likely he thought I was going to go all the way up there (up in the mountains near the Virginia border) and just sit on the bank while he fished. We'll take care of that, he says, and opens the door for me. Erlichman has a nice car. Like I said, the way he can be most of the time, I'm always surprised by his good taste. It's a little black Toyota Celica, but he can't drive it. The minute he pulls out in the traffic, pretty light since it's only about one fifteen, he starts jumping from lane to lane, passing on the right, cutting through gas stations and parking lots to miss a light (it's against the law, you know), making everybody else put on the brakes for him.

And then he starts telling me this sad story about how he and another low rate Realtor, Paxton—I've met him, what a dip—had been planning this fishing trip since last fall and now at the last minute Paxton backs out on him and takes a date to Atlanta to stay in the Peachtree and see some basketball game. How does he think this makes me feel? He doesn't think though, just pulls into a K-Mart and runs in, leaving me to wait twenty minutes in the car, and taking the keys off with him, so I can't even listen to the radio or tape player.

Just like with the shoes, I say to myself, why don't I just get out of the car right here at K-Mart and call Janie? Well, she would be at work still since it's Friday. And her parents are coming. And my bag is locked in the trunk. And just then here comes Erlichman out with a big plastic bag with one of those little four-foot long fishing poles that you buy for a kid sticking out. There is some other stuff in the bag like some floats and hooks and a jar of cheese flavored salmon eggs which trout really like, he tells me.

We get out on the Interstate (north on seventy-seven) when Erlichman gets this wild hair and cuts up an exit ramp. Let's go up the back way, he says. It's OK with me how we go just as long as we get there without getting killed. But Erlichman wants to go up old twenty-one just so he can show off a little, driving the car, down shifting and up shifting and letting his rear end hang over the yellow line on the curves because, like I said, he can't drive. Me, I'm kind of liking it, getting to play the radio on any kind of station I want since he's too busy acting like Richard Petty or Bobby Allison or somebody from Europe more likely since he says stock car racing is redneck and won't go near one (a race). And I like going through all the little towns like Cornelius and Davidson and Mooresville. You still see people on the sidewalk, not like Charlotte where it's cars, cars, cars. Sometimes they turn their heads and watch us go by in Erlichman's flash car, but mostly they are walking and talking about the weather and who's in the hospital and what to take to the cover dish supper.

After Statesville, I am getting nervous. I look at the clock on the dash (that will tell you what Erlichman is like—he took his car into the garage when the clock broke and got it fixed). It's almost four, and I wonder what Momma and Daddy are doing just now. The crops are in the ground, whatever Daddy planted this year besides his little tobacco allotment. Daddy will be in his dungaree jacket (the long kind with the ugly brown lining, not the cowboy kind), and he will be doing one of the stupid things that take up all of his time, like breaking down the engine on the tractor, trying to fix it himself when he doesn't know a blessed thing about it and in two days will have to call somebody like Uncle Leonard to help him. And mother will be...maybe sitting down. She's going to lose her leg, I know it. One day she just turned diabetic, in the middle of life with nothing ever the matter with her before. And now she won't watch herself and stick to her diet. It's hard, Daddy being picky the way he is, and because the way mother was raised the man always comes first. The last time I saw her, it (the leg) was all puffy and hurt. She wouldn't say so, but you could tell it. And that was back at Christmas time I'm ashamed to say, them living so close by. I don't know, it's just that when I go home it's all these questions about when I'm going to get married and come on home and start acting sensible. You know.

Now here's Harmony and off the road on the left is the little doctor's office with the fish picture, but the doctor is dead, and Harmony doesn't have a doctor now and, of course, we never did, so everybody has to go to Statesville or if it's serious to Winston or Charlotte. And that is where I was born: in the very examination room where the doctor sterilized the needles, and Momma delivered me with no drugs or pain-killers at all. It was a long labor. Momma will tell you all these modern women who are going in for this natural childbirth don't know what they're in for. She should know. And it must have been bad because after me there weren't any more. I'm her only baby.

Welcome to Welcome, I say just before we go around the curve where the sign is going to be. As soon as Erlichman sees it he looks over at me as if to say, well, ain't you smart. I grew up here, I say. Bullshit, he says. He never wants to believe anything anybody else says. I tell him that shows what a liar he is. He never denies it. I did really, I say, and then I see Uncle Leonard's old blue Ford truck cutting up the road to his and our houses. I can't see him really, just the truck, but I can see him in my mind with his greasy red hunting cap on and his dungaree coat just like Daddy's. I point our road out to Erilchman, saying, that's where I grew up. He says, that road looks like it goes straight to nowhere. When did your folks leave this hole? he wants to know. When I tell him they're still here, he says, well, hell, let's go see them, slowing down and getting ready to pull one of his fancy Charlotte driving U-turns.

No, I say, let's just go on. I couldn't stand it, taking Erlichman in Momma's house, her and Daddy making fools of themselves being polite. And Momma apologizing all over herself for the way the house looks and for not having anything cooked up for us as if she was supposed to have ESP. And Erlichman, although he would be polite and not say anything, would be looking around at Momma's best and having the same sneer going on in his head like he does when he comes to my complex. Worst of all having everybody in Welcome calling up Momma for the next three days, seeing a strange car and all, and Aunt Mabel probably seeing Erlichman and all of them thinking this must be it—Crystal has a fiancé. Momma would half way be believing it herself, even without me saying a word. Erlichman and me, that's a good one.

I squeeze over by the door wanting to be by myself as much as you can be riding in a car with somebody. Erlichman has to pick this moment to start getting cute, you're just a barefoot country girl, a farm girl. Yeah, I say just to get him to lay off me. I'll bet you've been up every road around here, he says and reaches over and gooses me. Yeah, I say again real soft, thinking how we used to run up and down the back roads where there weren't any cops, laws we used to call them, all weekend. And Richard, another thing I didn't want to get started remembering, in his '59 Impala driving like a crazy man—like Erlichman wishes he could.

I'll bet you knew all the best places where you could pull off and climb in the back seat, too, he says. We were in love, I say, surprised at myself. Erlichman doesn't say anything, not even something smart like who is we. We were in love, Richard and me.

Richard. He was a senior when I was just a little bitty freshman. But that's the way it always seemed to be at our school. The freshman boys were so dumb, still wanting to chase around the school house and punch each other in the arm. It was a big school, not what you're probably thinking, a big county school. But we were still all country kids. Momma and I used to fight all the time about me wanting to wear hose so much and me tearing them up running into the corners of the desks and the bus seats. And then riding to school with Richard in the big white Impala, driving like crazy. And Momma saying all the time, I don't care about you riding with him, but you're not going out with him, he's too old. Me sneaking until she gave up on it.

He was already drinking then. I wouldn't touch it. I'd even tell him things like I'll never marry a drinker, and make him promise he wouldn't drink before he came to get me. But he would still be a little drunk, and we would fight—it seems like we fought all the time. I would cry, and we would make up and then pull off (we'd been driving around all the time, that's about all we did was drive around and talk, about school, bitch about our moms and start making out). I loved kissing him, his mouth was always hot with the taste of cheap liquor or home-brew, but I was scared of everything else. He would start putting his hand under my blouse, rubbing my back and then come around and slide it up under my bra. I felt so pinched up with my bra being so tight to begin with without his hand there, me worrying all the time if I wasn't too small, that I didn't feel a thing. After a while, he would want to go up my skirt, and I would always say no, and he would act mad, but he would stop. That broke the spell I guess you could call it. We'd straighten up our clothes and he'd drive me home in the cold dark—I was always cold afterwards—without even the radio on. I used to think that was what it felt like to be buried in the wet ground like they used to do our ancestors with no coffins or anything.

Erlichman keeps looking over at me trying to make me look at him. I'll bet you never have even been in love, I tell him. Yeah I have, he says, and he starts telling me about her looks, like I want to know about her hair and eyes and what big boobs she had. If she was all that why did you leave her, I say to him, not guessing until after it is out of my mouth that it's her that left him. Erlichman gives me this funny

40

look—surprised just for a second, then he thinks I did it on purpose. She was a bitch, he says.

That's what broke you up? I say.

Ha, he says, it was just a stupid thing. I was supposed to go over to her place and water some plants while she went out of town. I didn't and some of them died. That should give you some idea of what she was like.

I don't blame her a bit, I say just to be mean. But Erlichman is pissed off about it now—more pissed off thinking about her than at me, and he's started taking it out on the car, driving stupid now, jerking it all over the road, red-lining it on the tach, and speeding of course. We meet the cop right on the crest of a hill. I look around in time to see him whipping his car around. Erlichman just lets off on the gas and takes it over onto the shoulder. Goody, I think, watching him walk back to the cop car with its big speed gun hung out the window, then God, what kind of weekend is it going to be now?

Erlichman tries to be nice by saying it's not my fault and all, but he still acts like it anyway, not saying anything and reaching over and flipping off the radio after a few miles. Even going the speed limit seems like a funeral now. Then we get up on the Blue Ridge Parkway. I've never been on it before. We always thought it was full of laws and just for rich people to ride on in Lincolns and Cadillacs. The sun is going down so pretty out in the west; I wish Erlichman would pull off so we could watch it. I need to go to the bathroom, I say. We'll be at the lodge soon, he says. When we get there, it's dark and there isn't even a TV in the room.

Like a dummy I just packed this shortie nightgown with an empire waist that makes the most of what little bit I've got. Erlichman, though, has been such a prick that I don't want to go out of the bathroom now. Getting in that bed is going to make me feel like a whore.

Erlichman doesn't even look up when I finally come out and sneak over to crawl in bed, all starchy and white inside. He's got his fishing junk spread out all over the floor sort of marvelling over it like it's Christmas morning, and it's the

41

first time he's ever seen it. Hey Erlichman, I ask him, me just sitting there without a magazine to read or anything while he plays with his flies, did you bring anything to smoke? I don't smoke much except when Erlichman has it. It makes me feel less nervous around him, but I wouldn't even know how to go about buying some.

You mean marijuana? he says like he doesn't kow what I'm talking about. Then he starts on all this junk about how you don't need it when you are going out in the woods and are going to get all high looking at nature. What is he talking about? I wonder, thinking about how ever since I was a kid Daddy and Uncle Leonard used to sneak off a couple of times each summer to set out a trot line on the Catawba River but mostly just to get drunk and lie around in the boat all night. And even Richard and the high school boys taking their fishing rods down to the river and building a fire, drinking and not even getting a line in the water. I know about fishing.

I remember waking up when Erlichman gets in bed beside me and says something about rising early. Then he turns his back on me and goes to sleep, not so much as a good night for me. I can't get back to sleep.

Naturally I'm thinking about Richard, how it was when he went to the Marines and came back with all his hair cut off. And me sitting on the front porch every afternoon without a thing to do but think about him until I missed him so much that I could feel it down in my womb, as Momma calls it. Poor thing, I don't think she even knows the real name for it, much less any of the dirty ones—well, maybe those. But me just feeling empty and hollow down there and knowing when he came home I was going to give it to him.

He didn't know what to think, me slipping out of the house without a bra on under my sweater. So when he got to that part, reaching up under my sweater and finding nothing but pure bare skin, it took his breath away. Oh God, he said, and hearing him say it that way, like church almost, let me know he loved me. Then I was sure and not scared anymore. Even my breasts, the way it felt pulling my sweater over my head and skin to skin like that for the first time ever, like they weren't all the way hooked up to my body before. Feeling hot and wet down between my legs, just like inside his mouth, I let him have it.

It worked the very first time. I came right down to my fingers and toes. And I always did up until the very end when I could tell he didn't love me, when he ran his rough old hands all over me like he was washing his car, and kissing me too hard. It made me want to throw up, him telling me the last night of his leave we were through, that he could fuck me all week, me taking all the chances, and then kiss me off. But I just cried instead.

And now here I am again crying in the bed, Erlichman with his butt pointed towards me never hearing a thing. So I just lie there crying and feeling sorry for myself until I fall asleep which is not for a long time.

There aren't any deer outside the lodge, of course. I knew it all along. When Erlichman pulls the curtain over the sliding door just past daylight, all that's there is a big meadow leading to the woods and a bunch of white stupid looking cows around a salt lick. There's no breakfast in the room either, just a kind of café-restaurant on the other side of the Parkway from the lodge. The eggs there look for all the world (and taste like it too) like they were made out of rubber.

Erlichman is so excited that he doesn't bother to think how stupid it looks when we head across the pasture dodging the cow pies, him with his wading boots, and net and creel and rod in a little cover, and all the rest, and me with my white plastic K-Mart bag.

It's a couple of miles to the creek, Erlichman says. I don't think that means anything to either of us when he says it. But a couple of miles in the woods turns out to be a long way. It's all downhill, too, which makes the backs of my legs hurt and makes me wonder how we will ever get back up. Erlichman is like a kid, hiking along like Daniel Boone, not even noticing that I have to run every few yards to keep up with him. I can hear the water already, he says like he's been saying almost since we started. I think it's the leaves on the trees, but don't say anything about it. Poor Erlichman, he's got it in his mind like it's going to be something straight out of a beer commercial (except we don't have any beer so he can keep it holy or whatever), one of those commercials where they're (always a bunch of guys) pulling them in like crazy and finally the camera goes back and it looks like it's all taking place inside a glass of beer.

But I think it's going to be more like the fishing calendar pictures in the barbershop where I used to sit and wait every other Saturday for Daddy to get his hair cut. There was always a fat, dumb fisherman, not looking much like Erlichman but having all the same gear, with his line all tangled up in the trees and his hip boots caught on a barbed wire fence and his grandpa-looking glasses about to fall down his nose. Up the creek, all his buddies are laughing at him. I might as well tell you, you could guess anyhow, that's the way it turns out for Erlichman. The creek when we get to it, and I just fall down by it half dead, and Erlichman not even wanting to get out the lunch—we've got to save it, he says, is so skinny that when Erlichman finally gets his long rod put together, it will just about reach clear across the creek. He puts on his waders and arranges all his junk on him and then tries to cast out, like cracking a whip. And sure enough, he gets hung up right off. So he sloshes across the creek and gets himself loose and says I can have this place and he will go on up the creek and see me later.

Thanks, after you already scared all the fish off, I say. I wasn't born yesterday. They'll all come back when they smell those salmon eggs, he says and fixes one on the baby rod I have, sets the float and casts it out for me. See how it's done? he says and then takes off without even bothering to see whether I do or not. Anybody can cast a fishing rod, I say after him, and even catch a fish. They're dumb, you know, dumber than chickens.

It's really kind of a pretty place, where Erlichman has dumped me. The woods come right up to the creek, but most of the trees are high up, and a big bank of mountain laurel on the other side where Erlichman got tangled up. There are some pretty big rocks up at the far end of this pool where the water spins through and makes a deep place that gradually gets shallower and kind of sandy down at the low end where the creek runs over a flat rock and then goes on. The water, even in the deep part is clear as glass. I can even see some fish, minnows like little transparent needles, swimming around, pecking at my salmon egg and making the float jiggle. Not a one of them could get the hook in his mouth if he had to. But they eat up the egg, so I reel in and put on another one, then can't get the line to cast out until I figure out you have to push the white button on the back of the reel. I knew anybody could do it. The minnows come around again, and I jerk the line to shoo them off, but they always come back. I put on more salmon eggs, and these little fish get braver all the time, tearing the egg to pieces, then darting around in a bunch looking for more. I take some of the eggs in my hand and shoot them out into the pool like marbles. The minnows go crazy tearing them to pieces. Then a weird thing happens. This one salmon egg falls right in the middle of them, but they all back away and let it fall down toward the bottom where all of a sudden a big gray fish rises up from in between a couple of rocks and eats it in one bite. Then he's gone, and there are only a couple of specks of that brown stuff that gets on river rocks swirling in the water to even let me know for sure that he was there. But he was there, and I'm thinking how he must have been sitting down there all the time, just watching. I feel cold and sort of nervous thinking about the way that fish just popped out. Erlichman, I say out loud. He can't hear me, of course, and I start to yell to him but stop and think that he would be mad as hell when he found out what I wanted, which was that a fish ate a salmon egg and scared me.

But now I want to be with him, so I start up the creek bank in his direction, just leaving my rod and salmon eggs by the water. I haven't gone far when I come to the second weird thing: It's a big round millstone—the kind that country people put beside their driveways sometimes with an X cut in the middle where the axle went. Here it is just sitting beside the pathway down here in the woods, miles away from people. And I start to think how people lived here, even way back a long time ago—all this before I even see the chimney. The chimney is on up the bank away from the creek. I go up to it, hearing Momma's voice in my head saying, be careful, that's just the place for copperheads. And I am careful, stepping over the threshold stone into the place that was once the cabin, all full up with pokeberry bushes and milkweeds and briars. There are still some rotten pieces of wood left, and I step over them easy-like, watching for those snakes, and get on over to the chimney and sit down on the hearth. I can see the little branch that runs just behind the house and down to the creek where they must have made their spring house. And how it must have been in those times to sit on the hearth at night just like I am doing now and listen to the wind in the trees and think, was that a bobcat? Was it a mountain lion going to come off the mountain and jump on the cow's neck? What would we do?

But inside, it would be warm, hot really, from the big fire of red oak. And I could have a big old pot full of rabbit stew. (Only I can't cook so good and skinning out some old rabbit would make me throw up. It was different then, though, I could have done it.) And over in the corner would be the old iron bed, Grandma's bed. It probably had to come up here on a borrowed wagon with a mule pulling it, and everything we owned would be in that one wagon. The old rocking chair, too, tied up on top of everything else. I would walk behind and lead the cow. And when the work was done and the bar put across the door so that no wild animals got in here, we would get in the feather bed. And who would get in that bed with me? Nobody I know. Not Erlichman, that's for sure. Richard? Richard could have gotten in that bed. Maybe it would have worked out that way, too, if he hadn't of fallen in love with city girls and fixing helicopter motors. After California, there just wasn't much in old Welcome to hold him, but here in the woods it would have been different.

I get up and walk out of the cabin right through the wall. I feel worse than after the big fish now, but it's nothing Erlichman can help, so I just go on back to where my fishing

46

pole is. There are still some blooms on the laurel, maybe because we're down in a hole where the days are so short. I think maybe I can cross the creek and get some for my cabin, ha ha. No, they are pretty and maybe I can put them in the K-Mart bag and carry them back up to the lodge and put them in some water. I take off my sneakers and socks and push my jeans up over my calves so I can wade across the pool down at the shallow end. But there are some slick rocks in the middle, and the water is so cold I know I'll just freeze to death if I fall in and get my clothes wet. But I still want the flowers. What the heck I say, there's nobody here but me (and Erlichman, but I'm nothing new to him) so I just pull my clothes off and fold them nice and neat with my underwear on top and start back across the creek. The water is so cold that when I get on the other side I see my feet and ankles steaming but it feels good. After I get the flowers and start back across, I say what the heck again and wade out to my thighs in the pool and scatter the big laurel blossoms around in the water and hold my breath and push out into the water the rest of the way like some Tahitian maid except that I have blond hair (light brown, really with blond highlights).

The water is so cold it takes my breath away at first. Then I feel nothing, just numb. I swim down to the big rocks and climb out on one, and suddenly it's like I'm on fire, and I can feel every inch of my skin all at once. It's just like the old light switch we had back home in the bathroom, the kind where you pulled a chain up by the light bulb. Ours had a short in it and whenever you touched it, a little shock of electricity ran all over your body. It was that way coming with Richard too—coming down in my soul and having it run out to my fingers and toes. Then just feeling limp all over, limp and warm. My nipples are sticking up, too, and I feel it there, too, and down between my legs. I ball up and let the sun hit warm on my back. I'm horny now and wish Erlichman would come back even though it's not really the same. Erlichman is good enough in bed, it's one of the things he takes pride in, like his car and his clothes. I come with him but it stays down between my legs and goes away pretty soon. It's never gone out to my fingers and toes except with Richard and that has been more than ten years. I used to say, was it me, but no, I am the same, have watched my diet and gone to Roman Health Spa twice a week and except for a little weight on my thighs, I am the same. It's not just Erlichman's ways, either. Some of the other guys (some I'm even ashamed to admit to, if I saw them on the street I would run in a store and hide) were a little better, but most were worse. I'm almost thirty—not yet, but close enough—and I wonder when it will happen again like with Richard.

Now that I am out on the rock and all warm and dry from the sun, I don't want to get back in and get the flowers. That's ok, they're coming apart anyway. I decide to just let them go down the creek, maybe they'll surprise somebody down there—somebody in a stinky mill town might have a nice day.

Then the third weird thing happens. I put my clothes back on and start walking around, just waiting really until Erlichman comes back, still kind of horny but more disgusted with Erlichman for not being around when I need him, for leaving me out in the woods like this in the first place. On our side of the creek the pine needles are really thick, like a shag carpet, all over the place, I walk around looking for something to do. Then I see it, a grave, right next to the path we walked down the hill on. We must have walked right past it and not even seen it. It's a girl, just a girl, and her name is the same as mine, well almost. Her name is Annie Dawson and mine is Crystal Ann Ellis. 1899-1914 it says on the limestone slab, already wearing away so you can hardly read it. There's a little rock dove with its head broken off on top of the slab, and some more writing under the date, Dear Wife. O God, I say, just a poor baby and married already and then dead so fast. I go closer and squat down next to the stone, being careful not to get on the little dip in the dirt where the body must be. Still I think, just fifteen, and she already did more than me.

I cry and think about Annie Dawson and how she must have had everything in the world, her little cabin and a cow

48

and a stout husband who could go out in the woods and shoot a deer for their dinner and catch fish out in the creek. And what became of him? Digging this very grave himself to kill the grief I bet and then sometime later, probably in the spring, because she would have died in the winter of pneumonia or some wasting disease, after sitting by the fire just watching the flames and barely eating enough to live, going down the mountain to town and buying the stone and borrowing the same mule and bring it up here on its back. Then just leaving, not even cleaning out the cabin, and letting everything fall down to just the way it is today.

When Erlichman comes back down the creek, he's holding his rod out away from him, trying to keep it away like it smells bad, blaming everything on his equipment. Now it's like I see him as a little boy. I want to talk to him in baby talk just to tease him, but I don't.

I found where somebody's buried, I tell him and his eyes get round, him thinking of somebody with their head stove in by a sledgehammer that will get our names in the paper. With a tombstone, I say and take him to see it. He looks for a minute and says, let's eat lunch and get out of here, they aren't biting. She was married, I tell him. Probably what killed her, he says with his mouth full of sandwich.

Going back up the hill is pure-t hell, straight up and Erlichman being mad and all. We don't even stop to rest, just walk and sweat until my hair is coming down in my face, and it feels like I have little sticks and pieces of leaves all under my clothes and in my shoes. My mind just goes blank, otherwise I would have never made it. On top the wind is cutting like a knife, and I have to pee real bad, so I take the room key and run down through the pasture, trying to watch out for the cow pies and back to the lodge. I wish there was some satisfaction in getting to the top, but there's not.

I look out the sliding window to the balcony and see Erlichman coming down the pasture all stooped and weak, now looking much like a broken down old man as he did a kid a while ago. I don't like him either way, I decide. But I go on out to help him with his junk anyhow.

49

Let's go get some gas before the station closes, he says, we want to get away tomorrow early. So we go across the road to where we bought our breakfast. When Erlichman pulls up at the station, the high school kid who runs the pumps about wets his pants looking at that car. But I go inside the station where there's a fat lady in a forest ranger shirt and a brown skirt working behind a souvenir counter.

They have little necklaces and rings made out of garnets which is my birthstone, and I'm thinking how nice it would be if Erlichman would buy me one. He won't, of course. They come from right out in the woods around here, the garnets, says the lady behind the counter. Oh, I say. I don't much like her. She has a tough face with a big jaw sticking out like my third grade teacher who was always saying, I can see right through you, honey. Staying up at the lodge, she says, you and your husband? He's not my husband I want to tell her, but I can't just like I could never face up to my third grade teacher and say about my spelling lesson, no, because I just don't want to do it. Yeah, I say. Then she looks at me like she knows I'm lying anyway, so why even ask me? I want to leave but I stay just to show her.

After a while I say, have you lived around here long? All my life, she says with her bulldog smile. Do you know about the grave down by the creek? Yeah, she says, the Liddel girl, married a Dawson. Drowned one spring when the creek was up. Washed her to that very spot where she's buried. Her man just dug the hole right beside the body and pushed her in. What happened to him? I say. Oh, he sold liquor for a good while, got rich off it during prohibition, then burned himself up—smoking in bed was all they could ever figure out. Drunk, you could bet. She just stops and I can't think of anything else to say, so I just say, oh. I try to act interested in looking around the store so I can slip on out, then I put money in the Coke machine and don't get a Coke. She sees it and is already coming over to me. She opens the front of the machine and hands me a pop and says, when I was a little girl I used to go over to the Liddel place—her people are still around here—and look at Annie's picture. Pretty as a doll, and Dawson (it was the wedding picture) big enough to pick her up with his little finger. Her mother was still living then, and when she caught anybody looking at the picture, she would say, I never could understand why she done it. But I was a young girl then, not a tough old bird like I am now, and I could understand. Her and Dawson down on the creek living like pioneers in what was almost modern times. I would have done it. Now it seems so stupid and so long ago. She smiles like she's getting ready to bite and I go on out.

Erlichman and the kid have the hood up on the Toyota talking about God knows what. Maybe it will make him happy a little and make up for today some. Me, I walk over to the edge of the highway. It is getting dark now, that time of day when there's just enough light so white things seem to glow. I see my blouse glowing and then look out at the white line on the road, how it seems to sort of lift up off the high-way. I follow it where it goes, up and over the crest of the hill and out of sight. I'm thinking how all of this has always been so close by, even when I was growing up, and yet I never knew it was here.

Two O'Clock In The Afternoon

Dad was home from the hospital where he'd gone for only a few days. He'd passed out on the sidewalk in front of their grocery store and had been taken to the hospital for tests. The doctors said he had the beginnings of a stomach ulcer, nothing serious, that he should take it easy awhile and go back to work when he felt stronger.

So Dad sat on the front porch on the green glider while Mom minded the store. It was funny seeing him sitting here, funny seeing him at the house any time during the day except Sunday. And fun, too, because he wasn't sick or anything, just resting. When the boys came from school, he would put on his old gray Navy sweatshirt and black tennis shoes and play with them in the yard. The two boys were both too young to catch or pass the football very well, but Dad didn't mind. He had been a guard on the first football team ever in the town. That made him famous and also accounted for the fact that he couldn't pass the ball too well. The boys knew guards did not pass, or catch, or score touchdowns, but were still not sure what they did do.

On the last day of his vacation, Dad loaded up the cooler with pop and sandwiches and took the boys up to the old vacant lot. The school football field had been there before the war; now there was a new field and a new school. The old field was just weeds and junk, a place where older boys had fights. The brothers were not to go there. With their dad, though, it was OK.

The boys found out Dad could punt the ball far and drop kick it, too. But they were disappointed to hear he wasn't the kicker for the team.

"No, I wasn't the best," said Dad. "There was another man, Earl Walker. Once the coach put us all on the goal line and said, 'We're going to run sprints now, unless Earl can kick the ball sixty yards. If he does, we'll all go home.' Earl took the ball. We only had one ball; in those days one was enough. And Earl sent Hoss, the manager, down to stand on the midfield stripe so he could see how far to kick it, and let her fly... And then we all went home."

The younger boy ran down the field, calling back, "This far? This far?" until he was waist high in the weeds at the edge of the field.

Dad went to the car for the cooler, and they went to the big tree in the corner of the field to eat their lunch.

"At the end of every practice, this is where we'd come to have our pep talks and skull sessions. Then we would get in a line and run back to town with the coach behind us hollering."

"Your team was good, wasn't it, Dad?" asked the younger.

"We beat Wytheville and Northfork that year, and that was an accomplishment for a little school like ours."

"How come you never got to be a pro?"

"Because of the war, dope," his older brother answered.

"Yeah! That's right."

The brothers understood the war better than football because they would watch "Victory at Sea" every Sunday with their dad. The narrator would speak boldly about the exploits of brave sailors while the gray newsreels rolled footage of destroyer convoys or carrier planes limping home with broken landing gear. Then they'd watch "The Twentieth Century" if it was about a war or rockets or something else exciting. Once it was about the Battle of the Bulge and one of the neighbors was in it. Everyone waited and finally Dad shouted, "That looks like him!" A fuzzy figure fell into line and ran along with his patrol. Suddenly they all dove to the ground and stayed there.

"That's him? That's all?" the brothers cried.

"You could only see his butt," the older brother complained. He got smacked for that. Nonetheless, the brothers would have been happy to have their dad's backside on TV. Every week while watching "Victory at Sea," they would ask, "Is that your ship? How about that one?" Their father's ship never seemed to get in the picture.

"What did you do in the war?"

"He already said he was a cook, a cook in the Navy," snapped the older.

"I know, but what about when the Japs attacked? You couldn't go on cooking with everybody shooting, could you?"

"Everybody had a battle station. A horn would sound on the intercom, and we'd all run to our battle stations. And wait."

"What did you do?"

"I was a gunner's mate. I spotted and made sure he had plenty of ammunition."

"What's spotting?"

"You look out for enemy planes so the gunner can fire on them."

"You never had a gun of your own?" the younger one wanted to know.

"These were big guns like cannons or ack-ack guns, weren't they, Dad?"

"Yes. I didn't have a gun to carry around, if that's what you mean."

"So you never shot any Japs?" the younger asked dejectedly.

"No."

"But he did see Ted Williams bat, didn't you, Dad?"

"The Splendid Splinter they used to call him. Boston—that's where we first shipped out. And when we were there, just waiting for our orders, they would give us free tickets to the ball games. The bleachers were full of servicemen. Of course, the teams weren't much then. Ted Williams himself went to war soon after that. And he was in the Korean War, too, a great man."

"Mom says he spitted on people once."

"He had a temper. But it was something to see him play. He could hit to any field and play the wall in left field in Fenway Park better than any man before or since. He went three for five that day I saw him against the Cleveland Indians."

"What else happened to you?"

"Well, we saw the Boston Bruins play hockey once. And I went to places in New York when we tied up there, pier ninety-two, the Brooklyn Navy yard. Red Cross girls would come down every morning and pass out coffee and doughnuts. We all went just to see the girls. I saw Glen Miller uptown once and took your mother to see him on our honeymoon later."

"There weren't any Japs around New York, were there?" asked the younger one.

"They were in the Pacific," the older added. "So how did you get there?"

"First we went through the Panama Canal. It was sort of a shakedown cruise since we were all new sailors. They had a big dry dock there where ships could be pulled completely out of the water and worked on. Our ship was dry docked. The whole crew had to clean the barnacles off the sides. The other cooks and I would have to make sandwiches and pitchers of iced coffee and hand them down the sides on ropes all day. It was better than scraping barnacles, though. At night we went into town. They had parrots and monkeys there for sale—lots of tattoo parlors, too."

"How come you didn't get a tattoo?" asked the older.

"Your momma wouldn't have liked it."

"You weren't married then."

"I know, but I could tell she wouldn't."

"Get to the war," the younger interjected.

"First we had to cross the International Date Line. When you do, the day changes, just like that. Then you have to meet Davy Jones. You have to jump off the side of the ship and go down under it. We call that Davy Jones's Locker."

"Was he a ghost?"

"Sort of."

"Like the men they threw over the side in bags on 'Victory at Sea'?"

"Well no, not really. Those men were real. They were casualties. Davy Jones was just a legend. Anyway, everybody had to dive down or there wouldn't be any luck for the ship."

"Did you do a swan dive off the ship?" asked the older.

"No, the sides of the ship are high; you have to jump and be careful to land feet first. A belly smacker from that high up might be the end of you."

"Were there sharks?"

"Yes, but they would put a big net in the water so that it was just like a swimming pool."

"So you couldn't get hurt?"

"No, they wanted to keep us safe. At night, some nights, the Pacific would be so calm and blue that you could stand on the fantail and see the glowing wake churned up from the screws. It would glow green from the sea animals the propellers cut up."

"But where did you fight the Japs?"

"The ship I was on was a troop transport, a bus in a way. We hauled soldiers around to different islands in the Pacific, sometimes to combat, sometimes to leave."

"So you never had any big sea battles like on TV?"

"Our ship wasn't designed for that; we tried to stay out of trouble."

"Oh. Where did you take the soldiers?"

"Just little islands you've never heard of."

"Like where?"

"Well, Guadalcanal, Tarawa, Attu. . .But they weren't much fun. The fun places were Hawaii and Tahiti. Tahiti is the only place out there I'd ever want to go back to. When you boys grow up, I'm going to buy a Cadillac and go get me one of those dancing girls they had there and settle down. But don't tell your momma." He winked at them.

The next day, Dad's vacation was over. He went back to the store. The brothers passed and kicked the football by themselves but weren't any good like Earl Walker must have been. It was getting too cold to play outside anyway.

Every day as the afternoons got shorter, they got out their electric football set and played. The older one had the blue men and was the Baltimore Colts. The younger's were red, so he had to be the Redskins. They had football cards and named their players after them, though neither had enough Redskins or Colts to go around. They picked the meanest from the rest of the cards to fill the gaps.

One day the brothers came home from school and found their mother running up the stairs. The lady next door and the nurse from across the street were there, too. Their mom explained that Dad had taken some cold pills that had hurt his ulcer, and he was sick. They should stay in the living room.

They lay on the floor examining their football cards listlessly. The older one went through the cards and explained them to his brother: "Raymond Berry doesn't look like a football player, he looks like one of the engineers from over at the company office. And Johnny U. looks kind of humped over and dumb, but he's not. Gino Marchetti looks a little bit like Dad except his hair is already gray."

"He's old," agreed the younger. "But why does he just get to play on defense? Van down at the store gets to play all the time."

"That's different."

The neighbor lady hurried by with a bag of ice cubes and went up the steps. They stared after her. Suddenly their Dad shouted, "Twelve o'clock!" They looked up as if through the ceiling to the place where his bedroom was. He yelled out again, "Two o'clock!"

The two boys got up and moved to the stairs. They climbed to the landing together. There they saw the nurse and Mom holding ice bags to Dad's head and stomach. The neighbor lady spoke on the phone as calmly as she could to the ambulance man; he used to play football, too. Then she called the hopsital and told them who was coming. The nurse took the phone. She spoke in a low voice and told the people on the other end that Dad was hemorrhaging and in a delirium from the pills he took. The boys couldn't see any blood, though. "Charlie at two o'clock!" Dad cried again. He tossed and tore at the sheets. "Hit him!" he ordered.

The ambulance arrived and two neighbor men came running to help the attendants. They shooed the boys off the stairs. Then they put Dad on Mom's straight-backed sewing chair because the stairs were too narrow. The neighbor men carried him to the porch. Then they strapped him on a cot and carried him to the ambulance. Mom got in and the nurse, too, then they left. The siren was on wide open.

The brothers stood on the porch and looked off down the street until the neighbor lady took them inside and gave them cookies. She made them understand that their dad was mighty sick, but he wasn't going to die. They felt hungry when they heard that, as if they hadn't eaten all day. It was already dark, and they hadn't noticed.

"Dad was dreaming about the war, wasn't he?" the younger asked.

"I guess he was," said the neighbor lady.

The older one punched his brother. "Hush up," he whispered. They knew something now.

The Other Side Of Christiansburg

As soon as we pull off at the truck stop, I know what my wife's going to say:

"You know how I hate stopping at these places. Particularly around here."

But I've had just about all I can take of fog and sleet. And besides, she starts this junk every time we come up to my mother's. Whenever we get to Christiansburg she starts with, "These roads are so twisty," "I'm getting nauseated," and "Everything is so dreary around here." She's from Richmond and thinks the state ends at Roanoke. Meanwhile her dog is jumping all over the back seat, trying to get into the front seat, drooling all over the windows.

"Look," I tell her, "I've got to have some coffee unless you want to drive."

"You know I can't drive on these mountain roads."

"OK, then. We could have flown, you know, if you hadn't wanted to bring that neurotic animal along."

So she clams up, thinking I'm a son of a bitch. But I've got a nice car, a new Olds Cutlass, and I could have a Mercedes if I wanted to flaunt it. I make that kind of money. So I think I ought to be able to drive my car in peace and not have an Airedale blowing in my ear for three hundred miles.

Then just as we get through the door of this place, she says, "I don't want anything." The waitress has got to hear her.

"Suit yourself," I say. I want to call my mother anyway so she won't be driving herself crazy wondering where we are. I like the place, kind of an auntie-style truck stop, nice and clean, formica tables. I know they've got plate lunches with plenty of vegetables. No dirty magazines, pinball or beer. They've got a sign painted up on the back wall, "The Virginian Café" with a couple of cardinals as fat as chickens perched on the letters.

When I get through with the call, I see Jan in a corner booth, not even pretending to look at the menu. She starts arching her eyebrows and making other signs that women have when they are trying to get your attention in a subtle way.

"What is it?"

"That woman over there—don't look now—is giving you the eye," she tells me.

So what, I'm thinking. Jan picked me up right after work, so I'm still in a three piece suit. But I like to look sharp, even in my casual clothes. And just for the record, I never buy a suit off the rack anymore. There's nothing like a tailored fit. I get more wear out of them, too. "What do you expect," I tell her. "How many times do you think they get to see a guy dressed like me around here?"

"I'll bet she's one of your high school sweeties," she says, trying to be funny.

"Not likely, we're still fifty miles away from home," I tell her. But since I was figuring on getting the silent treatment while trying to drink my coffee, I decide to play along. I make a show of getting up to take off my coat and tie, sneaking a look at the woman. I have to sit down quickly. "It is somebody I know."

Jan loves it when she thinks I'm losing cool in public. "I'll bet she's one of those girls you left pregnant when you went off to college."

I feel pretty conspicuous sitting in an almost empty café talking about somebody sitting just across the room. So I slip over to the jukebox and, without paying much attention,

punch up some stale country sounds. I look up cautiously—
I don't want her to catch me looking at her—and see she's
staring a hole in her coffee cup. That's good, I think, she must
not want to meet me, either.

"So tell me about her," my wife says when I get back, "now
that you've strutted around the room so she can see you." I
didn't think I was strutting. And even if I was, so what? I wish
our old school had class reunions because I'll bet I'm the only
one in the class of mine who could say he hasn't gained a
pound since high school. And I'm in condition too; I jog and
do a sub-six mile, cut a good figure in my shorts.

"She looks like a whore," my wife says.

"She's not a whore. I don't think she looks like one. Her
name is Zenith Parker, and I used to be quite fond of her."

"I see," she says like she thinks she's on to something.

"Not like that," I tell her. "But I would have if she'd given
me a chance."

"I thought you made every girl in your class." My wife
resents it because I had a good time in high school and she
didn't. I did everything—sports, the band, clubs. My mother
kept a scrapbook of it all. I still get a kick out of looking
through it. And I had some girls, too.

But I tell Jan I never made it with Zenith Parker, even
though she was the best looking girl in our school. It's a sweet
memory I've got of Zenith, and I'd kind of like to keep it to
myself. But Jan just won't let it rest.

"OK," I say, giving in to her, "Zenith Parker was a year
ahead of me. She used to have study hall in the back of my
world history class. Her desk was the last one in the row by
the wall, mine was the last one in the row by the window."

"Love across a crowded room," Jan cuts in.

"I used to lay my head down on my desk and just gaze
across at her legs. God, she had good legs. This was back before
real miniskirts were in, but her skirts, especially her cheerleader skirt, were short. When she sat down I could see a good
six inches of leg above her knee."

Jan doesn't like this. She thinks I look at women too
much anyway. Everybody does it, I tell her. "Not me. Not

women. Women don't look at men," she says. That's not true, but I'll never get her to admit it. Besides, in those days I was considered to be a pretty wholesome guy. My friends wouldn't even sit in the back of the class. They liked to sit up front and look back down the aisle—shooting squirrels we called it. I guess Zenith was just a tease.

"I was just a sophomore then," I tell Jan, "and anyhow, she was going with a guy in the Air Force several years older than her. She had his ring, big as a golf ball, on a chain around her neck."

"So what's the point?"

"She knew I wasn't going to do anything. It was a cheap thrill."

"And that was nice?"

"I thought so," I tell her. The rest of it is all tied up with my old basketball days. I like to reminisce about them. Jan hates hearing about any of it by now, but I can't help it. How many times do you get to the top? I say you've got to relive them.

"When I was a sophomore I was getting to play a little in all the games. But when we were blowing people out, I got to play a whole half."

As expected, Jan starts complaining, "This isn't going to be another basketball story?"

But I can't help it. I'm excited now. Those particular memories are so distinct. I can even see myself in the picture, a good hook shot. I had it then. "We had just destroyed a team and I felt great. It was my first varsity game in double digits."

"The Hurley game," she says and tells me I'm just a big kid.

I don't care now. "I was bombing away," I go on, and then realize that I by-passed the part where Zenith came in. So I back up, "But then I noticed that she. . ."

"Zenith Parker," Jan adds.

"Yeah. She had stopped wearing that guy's ring. About three days before, I'd looked up and it was gone. She was carrying around a shredded Kleenex all the time and looking kind of red around the nose and eyes. I took those to be all the signs that she and that guy were through.

"I felt so good about that game I was whooping around the locker room feeling like a stud. For the first time, I began to put together the fact Zenith Parker didn't have a chain around her neck anymore with what the starters had been telling me—that I ought to be able to start coming on to women now that I was starting to come on as a player. I was sort of shy, but with those points under my belt, I felt like I could do something about it."

But now I'm thinking about a part of it that I wouldn't want to tell Jan. I imagine there are always things that go on in a man's life that he can't ever tell his wife if he wants her to respect him. Our team used to stop on all the away trips at a little roadhouse called Wimpy's at the top of Claypool Hill. It wasn't much of a place, a greasy grill and bottled drinks, nothing like the clean bright Virginian Café. But in the middle of a four hour bus ride home, it sure was a relief. The way things broke down, the cheerleaders sat at the tables in the middle of the floor with the sponsor, coach, and bus driver. The stag guys like me had to go to the counter. With fifty cents from the coach, we could get a burger and a coke. If we wanted something more we paid ourselves.

I guess I was jumping around a lot, bragging and shouting, doing just about anything that would get Zenith's attention. I remember trying to sing along with "Day Tripper" on the jukebox. Needless to say, I wasn't having much luck. So I started making a big show, like a magician, taking the tops off the salt and sugar containers and mixing up the contents. The waitress saw me and told the coach who took me outside and chewed me out and let me know it would be rough for me at practice Monday. We didn't get to stop at Wimpy's our next two games either.

Then Jan snaps at me. "What are you thinking about?" She wants to know what I'm thinking about any time I get quiet.

"Nothing," I tell her. "I was just thinking about how tight I used to get for those games."

"I want to hear about Zenith Parker," she demands.

I get a little put out with her bugging me. "There's not much more to say. I just went out to the bus by myself and when everybody else got on, I pulled her into the seat with me. We could sit with the cheerleaders after any game we won. If we played real well, the coach would keep the interior lights off the whole trip and stay in his seat. Zenith didn't know what to think of me. Neither did I. I don't know what I thought I was going to do, but I knew there was a deep cut in the mountain we'd have to go through. I figured I'd wait till that cut and make a move."

"A move?" Jan says.

"Yeah, a move. I didn't know much about the preliminaries then, so I decided that I would put my arm around Zenith as soon as we got into the cut and try what I could."

"Were you going to cup her boob or what?" she wants to know.

"At that point in my life, a wet kiss would have been more than enough. But I didn't even get that. It was too far to that damned cut and I didn't know what I was supposed to do in the meantime. 'Do you think we'll make the state play-offs this year?' I asked even though everybody was sure we would anyway. She said, 'You're going to college, David.' I couldn't figure out what that line was supposed to mean. But she said it real sisterly. I was missing all the signals."

"You always have," Jan tells me.

"Like what?" I want to know.

"Like the fact that that poor woman is sitting over there waiting for you to get up and say something to her."

"Yeah? A while ago she was a whore." But I go ahead with the story, "So we got to the cut and I got my arm around her and was turning around to kiss her when all of a sudden she reached up and grabbed me by the ear lobe, pressing so hard that she cut into it with her thumbnail. The she just pulled me up to her mouth and said in a firm voice, 'David, you're a sweet boy, but I swear if you don't get out of this seat I'll scream. I mean it—get gone.'"

At this my wife starts laughing like crazy, getting all red in the face. I'm afraid she's going to upset my coffee. And the half dozen people in the place are looking our way and seeing for the first time that we aren't their type. I've got to admit that I wish I didn't have this suit on now. But I try to play it cool and look around the café with a soft smile on my face, trying to let them all know that it's nothing against them or anything. When I see Zenith Parker, I see she's looking kind of hurt, like somehow she knows we're laughing about her. And I know that I'm going to have to talk to her before we get out of this place.

"I'd like to know what's so funny," I say to Jan in a whisper, though I know nobody could hear us over the juke box anyway.

"You!" she's gasping between laughs, "you got exactly what you deserved."

"That would make you happy, but that's not the whole story. I expected her to blab the thing around school for a week and make me the joke of the team. But as far as I know, she didn't tell a soul."

"And that was it?" she says, calming down and a little disappointed.

"Yeah. She asked to change her seat in my history class so I couldn't see her anymore and never smiled at me in the halls. But she danced with me at the prom and wrote that I was a sweet kid in my yearbook. I went to her wedding about two weeks after her graduation."

"Pregnant?"

"No. Just what she wanted."

"Well, that's quaint. I want to meet her."

"Why?"

"Because I think she ought to know that you're still carrying a flame for her twelve years after the fact." And she gets up and starts walking toward Zenith's table over near the counter. I have to hurry to get in front because Zenith is getting this scared, happy smile on her face like she thinks she's going to meet somebody special.

"Hey Zenith," I say, sort of shielding my wife off behind me.

"David, I knew it was you when I saw you walk in the door. You haven't changed a bit. I'm surprised you recognized me at all. I'm so fat now."

She's right. She hasn't blossomed out into one of those whales whose butt hangs over the sides of a bar stool, but she's put on a good forty pounds. And I know that Jan is rolling her eyes all over Zenith like a couple of cold eggs, giving her a superior sneer like women do to each other. Poor Zenith looks down at her lap just like she used to do in history class when she caught me staring. Then she used to blush a little like she felt sorry for me. Now it's the other way around.

"It was your smile," I say.

She's pretty nervous, scratching in her purse, "Looking for a cigarette." But she pulls out her wallet instead and starts showing some blurry Polaroid snapshots. "Here, here are my kids. Christmas, you can see the tree behind them. Tammy, that's the big one, is eleven now. Tracy, she's about eight and a half."

"Has it been that long?" I say, trying to sound sincere.

"Yeah, because, let's see...I was carrying Tammy that winter when you were a senior. I was sick with her the whole time. And lonely. Randy was driving the wrecker nights for the Citgo. He'd let me off at the schoolhouse. I saw every home game. You were so good. I knew you'd make it at college. I watched the papers."

"He was a substitute," my wife says.

"I was a little too short to play forward," I explain to Zenith. "But I was good as anybody coming off the bench."

Right now I can feel Jan glaring at me, letting me know I haven't introduced her. "This is my wife..."

"Jan," she finishes, putting her hand forward to shake. Zenith just looks back in her pocketbook for the cigarettes. "Randy is your husband? How is he?"

"He's in Delaware. We're divorced but he pays my alimony and child support. It's been so long. I was bu sy with the babies, and then the first thing I knew he was saying he was tired of me. And then he just left. But I don't say much against him now."

"That's terrible," my wife whines in her voice of feminine camaraderie.

"Well," says Zenith the way country women do when they consider the subject has been covered. "But David must be doing good."

I like this scene. Suddenly I'm out of the conversation and gettng treated like I was a picture Jan pulled out of her wallet.

"I do all right," I put in.

"Any kids?" Zenith asks, going right on with Janet, getting confident now that we're on this women's talk.

"We have this dog," I say before Jan can get into one of her long excuses about how we are still too involved in getting *our* business firmly established to start thinking about children.

"Say, Zenith," my wife says, "David's always telling me about what a lover boy he was back in high school. I'll bet you could set the record straight."

Jan thinks this will be some kind of joke on me. But Zenith only gets red and says, "We didn't have any classes together. I was a year ahead of Davd."

"Come on," says Jan (she never knows when to quit.). "What about all those long bus rides you used to take?"

Zenith shakes her head and looks away, smoking nervously.

Jan's really put her foot in it this time. And now that the damage is done she realizes it. She remembers that the dog has to have its walk and scoots out the door, assuring Zenith and me that we'll have a lot to talk about. We don't, not now.

"Your wife is pretty, so nice and slim."

"Yeah." Jan with all her down-east sophistication can't understand that what happened between Zenith and me could never be talked about. It was our secret, and exposing it to the open air could only ruin it. "Remember the good times," she hinted in my yearbook. That was enough; we both knew what she meant.

Now Zenith is sitting here all red and puffy, trying to get a good times conversation started. But I don't have the patience for it. I know it's not her fault she's crawling, trying to get around my suit, my trim wife, and the fact that I'm getting along better than she is.

I can see her belly bulging against the top of her puce pantsuit; it's not the best looking outfit I've seen. And her heavy make-up caked on her cheeks and the bridge of her nose, plus too much mascara, doesn't help either. But she made her choices. And I don't mean my little episode on the bus either, but the whole show. Anyway, I'm thinking the best thing to do is to clear out as quick as I can.

"Where are you living now," I say, bring the conversation up to the present in a flash.

"Bluefield."

I should have known. I can just about see the place, one of those new trailer parks thrown up on a shaved-off hilltop, a yard full of yellow mud every time it rains.

"What are you doing in here then?"

"I work at the Celanese plant. My ride got sick and went home early. I was hoping somebody would come by." I'm cussing myself mentally for getting stuck like this. But I decide to keep quiet and hope she'll let it pass.

But she says, "Are you on your way home, David?"

"Yeah, just for a day or so." I never could lie looking people in the face. "Mother's alone now and she's been a little sick," I throw in trying to make it sound like a desperate situation.

There's another silence and then she says, "David, couldn't you carry me as far as Bluefield since you're going that way?"

Trying to buy some time, I say, "I imagine Jan's getting a little impatient. It's pretty cold out there to be walking a dog." But Zenith just sits there waiting.

The truth is, I don't want Zenith in the car. There's nothing wrong with her. She's just a nuisance I don't want to put up with. I can't tell her that, so I say, "If Bluefield was any closer, I'd say sure. But that's forty miles. And it's the dog. It seems funny, I guess, not the kind of thing you would have seen around home when we were kids, letting a dog ride in the car and all. We make him stay in the back seat, but he's not well-behaved."

"I've ridden in a car with a dog before."

I stand there for a minute trying to think of an easier way to say no. Then I go for my wallet. I don't know how much coffee costs in a truck stop these days, but I'm going to leave a dollar. I don't want to wait around for change.

"Please," says Zenith in a soft, hoarse voice, right on the edge of crying. I look at her now and think how much she really does look like a whore. "You don't know what it's like to work all day in that stinky factory. Standing up. My feet hurt all the time. And I've been here five hours looking for a ride." I'm tempted to tell her that part of her problem is wearing those cheap shoes.

"Look," I say, "here's a twenty. I'm sure the bus comes by here. I'm sure I saw one of those Greyhound signs out front."

She just looks at me, her puffy face looking like a week-old balloon starting to go down.

"I know you could get somebody to take you for twenty bucks. It's just that my mother is going to be waiting up late as it is. I don't want to drive all over Bluefield."

I push the twenty to her, but she lets it fall on the floor. Then she's shaking so much she can't get her cigarette lit, so I have to do it for her.

"Are you going to take the money?" I ask her.

She looks away for a minute. Her mouth is working like she wants to say something but it won't come out. Then she says, "Piss in your eyes," and goes off to the bathroom.

I pick up the bill and put it back in my wallet and head out the door. I'm sorry for old Zenith, but she was stupid for not taking the money.

It really is getting colder outside. I'm heading for the car where Jan is getting the mutt into the back seat. I don't like a four door car, I don't like the lines cutting up the sheet metal like that. If people want to ride in the back, let them crawl over. There's not much room back there, even in an Olds. It's what they call a personal luxury car.

69

Now the sky is slate colored and the fog has lifted. It isn't going to sleet any more, it's going to be a good heavy snow. But I've got studded tires (they're illegal in Virginia, but I pay taxes don't I?), so we're OK. Sure enough, after about half an hour here come these nickel sized flakes, beautiful. The dog has settled down and is actually asleep. I look out on the snowflakes converging on us like galaxies of stars. I like the cockpit sensation I get from looking at the gauges in the faint green light of the dash. I can hear the steady cooking of the engine, the snow tires humming with authority. And I feel better. I guess weepy Zenith put a damper on my spirits.

"Dave?"

That irritates me. I thought she was dozing off. "What?"

"I think it was sweet the way your old girlfriend went to see you play all those games when you thought she'd forgotten all about you." Now Jan's trying to smooth it over, trying to pretend that everything was peachy back at the truck stop when she caused it all anyway.

"She wasn't my girlfriend. And she didn't come to those games because of me. What else was there for her to do at night?"

"Why would she say that then?"

"She just wanted something."

"What could that be?" Jan asks, coming on like she's appalled, as if women never want anything. "She could tell you'd amounted to something and wanted to be a part of it."

"I have amounted to something," I admit. "But she wanted something. Forget it."

"You're awful," she says, but at least she drops it. Then, "Ooo, it's snowing hard, Dave. Are we going to make it to your mother's? I hate this. I knew the weather would turn bad. You know we have to be back in Richmond for that party on the weekend."

"Go to sleep," I say and turn on the radio. Up here in the hills, there's not an FM station on the band. All I can get is country-western and top forty. I try this hillbilly station that still has the down home announcer handling all the commercials live, no canned stuff. "Let me tell you about the plate lunches you can get from the good folks down at the Virginian Café..." he says like an old pal.

Jan comes to life, "That's where we stopped." Just like a kid. I run the channel selector down the dial and look for something else. Right now, I can't stomach any country. But I'm not having any luck finding another station and it's getting annoying. Finally I switch the radio off and then I see the snow is starting to stick. It must be even colder than I thought.

"Dave?" I act like I don't hear her, but she goes on. "I think you're wrong about Zenith. I think it was you that made her want to come to those games. You remember the first time you ever brought me up here to meet your folks and told me about your high school games? You said they still had a picture of you in the trophy case getting the game ball after you scored your thousandth point."

"That was a few years ago. It's probably gone now."

"And you said that every fall when they gave out the uniforms that the high school boys would argue over who would get to wear your old number."

"That's partly true. But I'm not the only guy who ever wore that number."

"And you remember that you said on your graduation when the principal gave his speech that he singled you out and said that because you were at the head of your class and had gotten a basketball scholarship that people in town expected you to go out and make a name for yourself. Kids in your town who never thought about college would have an example to follow."

"Yes," I say and can see Jan's smile in the light of the dash. She thinks she's won this round. But what she doesn't know, what I didn't tell her is about the time before the first game of my senior season when the coach told me to step into his office a minute. I thought it was going to be a talk about how cigarettes would cut your wind, or about using a rubber and staying out of trouble.

Instead he said, "What do you think about the other guys on the team?"

"They're OK. I like them," I said.

"Well," he said, "as basketball players they aren't for shit. They do all right, and they'll do all right when they get out of here as miners or truck drivers or whatever. Don't worry about them. You've got some ability, you know that?"

I didn't know what he was getting at so I told him, "Some."

"You've got some...enough. So I'm telling you, don't screw up. Take what you can get, understand? Take it."

But I didn't understand exactly, not then. I didn't understand until the championship game of our district when we were two points back with a minute and a half to go and the rest of the team was standing around looking like they were going to pee in their pants. I scored six points and we won it—easy because the other team was as scared as we were. That minute and a half got me three college scholarship offers.

And I realized before I walked off the floor that night that I could be more than just another good ball player in a no stoplight town on the Virginia side of the coal fields. My coach told me right. I could get a long way in life by taking over when everybody else was gawking.

That's why I'm a success, as my wife loves to point out. And that's why I can pass through Bluefield and not even feel very guilty. People like Zenith are always going to be stuck on the side of the road somewhere.

We're almost home now. But on past Bluefield the roads are really bad. It looks like only a couple of cars have gone through ahead of us. My Cutlass is a city car, an automatic. It doesn't even have positive traction. Who needs it in Richmond? But I'm beginning to wish I had my Dad's old straight stick Chevy. It's going to take some luck to dodge all the pot holes and stay out of the ditches these last few miles.

"This is terrible," Jan editorializes.

"What do you expect?" I tell her. "They let everything up here go to pot. Just like that Zenith Parker running to fat. No wonder her husband left her. He probably got tired of his car going in the ditch, too."

Normally, she'd have something smart to say back to me after a remark like that, but she lets it go. Then she says, "Dave, your mother must be worried sick."

"What's that got to do with anything?" I want to know.

"I was only thinking that we could put a stop to all this nonsense. We could get her a nice apartment in Richmond. Close to us, but not too close. She's getting old, and we wouldn't have to make this terrible drive anymore."

It's an old argument of hers. I hear it every trip somewhere along the line. I've told Jan my roots are here. I even like pulling into town late at night just like we did on the school bus after a road trip. But that memory doesn't hold much for me right now, and thanks to Zenith, it never will.

The hole I hit is so jarring that I think we must have broken the axle. Something is rattling down there. The dog is back up, panting and slavering like mad; Jan is hanging on the armrest like she expects me to drive over the hill, and I'm thinking that the only mechanic in town is a crook.

Maybe we should get my mother that apartment, I'm thinking. It'd make life a lot simpler. I've travelled this road enough times.

Weasel's Daddy

I knew him a long time before I knew he was Weasel's daddy. I'd seen him and I was scared of him. On Saturday mornings, my own dad would make me run the gauntlet of men and high school boys who by ten o'clock were hanging all over the bridge and sidewalk down on the lower end of town. I would be on an errand, usually to the bank with the blue and gold bank bag held tight and eyes down when I got to the bridge where they'd be sitting, smoking and talking and flipping their butts into the coal black creek that barely ran through Powell's Bottom. I guess I was scared of all of them, but Weasel's daddy especially, who, careful in his dress and often in suit pants and white shirt, stood down by the gas pumps outside Pigg's Hardware and stared. When I was older I understood that it was the stare of a far-gone drunk seizing on anything to hold himself in the world around him, and that was what also accounted for the faintly wobbly quality in his posture, as if he might just float away.

Hardly a week went by that I didn't get some grief on my errands. But even then I knew not to say anything to my dad. I was big for my age and was expected to be able to take it. Then I came out of the bank one morning, the bag empty except for the stamped deposit book, and ran into an argument on the bridge between Weasel's daddy and another man, big and not so sober either. Weasel's daddy grabbed me on the shoulder as I tried to scoot past and held me. I felt his power in that one hand, a long tattooed dagger coming down his wrist onto the back. He was saying, "I'll show that even this boy can do it. Fifty dollars says he can."

"Go on. I'm betting with you, not the kid."

"I'll catch him if he falls. Yes or no? Take it or leave it."

He took it, and Weasel's daddy picked me up like I was nothing and set me on the rail of the bridge, flat and about four inches wide, and said, "Show him. Walk it. I've got you if you fall." I could feel the urgency in his grip on my calf where he steadied me until I found my balance and held my arms out, bank bag clutched in my left hand, like the acrobats on "Sealtest Circus." Then I walked. It was a fifteen foot fall into the creek with its water full of coal dirt and stinky with sewage. On the other side was Weasel's daddy, and fearing falling in either direction, I made it across. As soon as he let me down, I broke a sweat all over my body. By then most of the loafers and passers-by and even some people in cars were watching. They gave me a cheer and said, "Way to go kid," but I just skedaddled. I'm sure my dad got wind of it, but he never let on, and neither did I.

But as I said, I didn't know he was Weasel's daddy then; I didn't even know Weasel. By the end of the summer I would. One day he just appeared, coming over the hill on Church Street right into the middle of a game of Indian rubber. He was on a yellow bike and he broke right through the fielders, standing up off his seat and slamming on the coaster brake at about the patch in the road we used for second base in regular baseball and sliding all the way past the tarpaper shingle we put out to mark first and out-of-bounds. Then he sat there and had a good look at us, or rather made sure we had a good look at him. The yellow bike didn't have fenders or a chain guard, and it had black handle grips with black streamers, too. And it had *The Sleeper* spelled out in chrome plastic balls down the tank that went from the seat to the front forks. After he'd watched a couple of us bat through and could see we weren't going to ask him to play, he took off, swerving as close as he could to the batter's box. "Shit ass!

come back here and fight if you think you're so hot," the batter yelled as Weasel went around the corner without looking back.

"The Sleeper," I said.

And J. J. Pigg who was the oldest and our leader said, "It wasn't nothing but a Roadmaster painted up. Mine's better than that."

Not to my eyes it wasn't. And the rest of the summer when I rode around town with my dad helping deliver the orders, I'd see him like a goldfinch flying here and there, up alleys, down School House Hill, jumping out from behind parked cars. I figured he must live down in Powell's Alley or Maple Grove, rougher parts of town outside my range of solo exploration. He was still a mystery, and I had already made up my mind to come out of my shyness if I could meet him.

It happened in school, where the Weasel flunked back into my grade. Seeing him off the bike, grimy and frayed, I knew in a second he wasn't the kind of kid I was supposed to be hanging around with. The teacher, the same one that failed him the year before, tried to get off to a better start by having him lead us to the gym and the lunch room, as if we hadn't been going to school there four years already. But when we got to the gym that first day, Weasel stopped at the top of the short flight of stairs that led down to the floor. "Go ahead," said the teacher, calling him Charles—he wasn't even the Weasel yet, that came in high school—and the Weasel jumped, turning a full flip in the air before he hit. She sent him back to the room, and he missed recess the rest of the week. But I remember his look right then as he turned back to the rest of us who still stood at the top of the stairs, amazed. He was both proud and defiant, sticking out his banty rooster chest, then later stomping off up the hall cussing and muttering just low enough so the teacher could hear him but not make him out. She knocked him down; he bounced back and at the end of the year she passed him just to be rid of him, I guess.

Still, I couldn't get the bike out of my mind. In late fall, one of the last days we could go outside, I got up my nerve and went up to him where he sat on the fence, alone but not alone because we all admired him but couldn't get close, so we hung around him like a halo. "You've got a cool bike," I said.

"See this?" He pulled a blue piece of cut glass out of his pocket and held it out in the light. It looked like a jewel. "What'll you give me for it?"

"Something."

"Well, it's going to have to be special because this is valuable." The next day I took him the sombrero friends of my parents had brought me all the way from Mexico. "Hun," Weasel said, but he took it. When my mom saw the trade I'd made, she blessed me out but didn't paddle me, considering the stupid bargain I'd made to be lesson enough. But I made two more deals like that before Weasel finally said, "Come by my house this afternoon and I'll show you my bike."

After school the safety patrol marched us down the long cement steps two by two. At the end of the first flight, the kids from Maple Grove and Powell's Alley got to go home on their own. "Let's go," Weasel told me. Even though I wasn't supposed to go his way, I went; I wasn't going to miss out now. The fat girl patrolling there saw us and yelled at me to come back. Weasel started running, and so did I until we came to the first house, where we ducked behind and slapped ourselves against the wall like TV soldiers. The fat girl stood up on the hill yelling down at us, "Come on out. I saw you. I'm going to tell anyway." I started to move away from the wall, ready to go out in the open and surrender myself. "Baby. She didn't see you, not to know who you are. If she did she would have shut up and turned you in." Scared as I was, I knew he was right and was wondering if all my trading was now going to come to nothing. Then we, after a few minutes' wait so I could make sure she wasn't going to come down after us— "That Jello?" Weasel sneered—cut diagonally across the yard, climbed that fence and another, taking the short cuts and precautions to Weasel's house.

I had always wondered whose it was. There were all these wooden toys, I guess you'd call them, set around in the yard, little windmills with real spinning blades, flying ducks whose wings looked more like propellers when they were standing still, and down on the ground, wooden cutouts of squads of ducks and grazing rabbits, all homemade and hand painted. "You make these?" I asked Weasel. "Sure, come on." And we went along the side of the house, where I thought I saw his mother, like a ghost at the window, to the shed that was built onto the side of some old company houses. Weasel pulled open the lock-less hasp and there it was, *The Sleeper.* I tried to act like I wasn't disappointed; up close you could see the brush marks in the paint and some of the dime store beads that spelled the name, placed crooked, were already coming off. But Weasel sensed it anyway. "It's nothing much now. The summer's the time for bikes. I'll probably fix it up again, then paint it a new color and think up a new name."

"Yeah," I said and looked around the rest of the shed where there were some old looking, but worn shiny, carpenter's tools. What really interested me though was a big four foot high rolling tool chest with drawers like a dresser that took up most of the back wall of the shed. Weasel, the proud owner, went over and pulled out the top drawer full of sockets and handles, then the succeeding others full of just about every kind of tool you could imagine—including the strange hammers and dollies for body work—lumps of steel, caveman's tools, I was thinking. "I could build me a car with all this stuff if I wanted to," Weasel told me and began assembling one of the sockets on a ratchet handle and extension. Then he stopped and listened, a look on his face that made me listen, too—I finally heard the steps on the wooden walk.

The man opened the door and stood in it. "Uh hun," was all he said, and I snuck out under the arm he had propped on the door jamb. So that was Weasel's daddy. I didn't look back but knew the door shut behind me.

Weasel skipped school the next day, but when he did come back he still had the look of a beating on his face. I didn't get a chance to talk to him until lunch, when he took his tray way down to the end of the table. I went and sat beside him and after the blessing said, "Your old man's crazy," thinking it would be the brotherly thing. "Bastard," he said and stuck his fist in my ear. We didn't get to fight long since all the teachers were right there, but it was long enough to know he could have whipped me pretty bad. I got sent home to change my clothes from where I got pushed down into my tray, and Weasel got sent home for the day. That was it between us until the ninth grade.

But Powell's Bottom, ringed around by the worn out mountains, made it impossible to get away from him completely. His mom still came in the store and bought her little dabs and carried them home in twelve pound bags. His daddy still stood by the gas pumps. (He would later make the slow migration up the street to the cool rest of Posi's place and then finally to the dirty steps in the alley behind our store where he drank straight out of the bottles from the liquor store a few doors away.) And Weasel himself stayed in my class, somebody I might run into on the Saturday sidewalk, and now a bigger threat than his dad. Hadn't he, even as they were pulling us away from the fight, me feeling just as glad it was over, yelled over his shoulder that he'd get me yet, just wait?

He would have his chance on the basketball floor. But before that I would grow up some more, so that I wasn't so shy as to keep my eyes to the ground on the way to the bank. The basketball fever was on Powell's Bottom just then; the high school team was winning and the town identity was tied up in the district title and even beyond. I heard the loafers comment on my height and the promise of another basketball generation coming along, so I started to believe like they did that Powell's Bottom and basketball would always be talked of together.

I also heard other things, like the story of Weasel's daddy and the fifty-seven Mercury, which, after watching my dad's face when we delivered the groceries, I knew to be true. It was the kind of car you had to love or hate, a big top-of-the-line Turnpike Cruiser with a 290 horsepower engine. But besides the outrageous styling of all fifty-seven Mercurys, as if the designers thought about fins but decided everybody

else had them and just shaved them off, Weasel's daddy's was
lilac and black, special ordered I'm sure, helped along by the
gold trim down the back fenders to the tail lights and two
wiggling hula girls in the back window. I loved that car as
much as Weasel's daddy must have. It was one of the highlights
of the delivery day to go down to Maple Grove and see it in
its shining splendor, wide whitewalls and waxed until it
glowed. Then one Saturday morning, Weasel's daddy came
out to find a flat on the left front tire, went up and kicked
the daylights out of it, which did nothing more than spring
the hubcap so it rolled into the street. Then, according to the
story, he just picked up the hubcap, opened the door and
threw it on the seat, said, "The hell with this," and walked off
to town. And that's the way it sat for five years with its flat
on the front as the other three gradually went down to join
it. The wax wore off, the paint faded and rust grew in spots
around the wheel wells and rocker panels. My dad grinned a
little every time he saw it.

Which doesn't go too far in explaining how it was between
my dad and Weasel's. How he, my dad, went up and dragged
him out of his booth in Posi's, where in the daytime nobody
even bothered to play the jukebox, to come and fix our back
porch. Weasel's daddy hadn't had work since he got fired from
the Pigg's Ford place for coming in drunk, and that had been
a while. Most, including my mother, said he didn't even try
to find work. But he came when my dad asked him, showing
up with those same old carpenter's tools in a canvas bag. For
several days I watched him from the kitchen and back yard.
I was scared at first, but then I saw that even if he remembered me from the bridge or his tool shed, he pretended not
to. It was he who'd changed, lost the crease in his pants and
his clean white shirt, and taken on a pissy smell. He did his
work slowly, without even a song, only cussing when he
dropped a nail or one of his tools, which seemed pretty often.
Then he swept up the sawdust, looked at his job, shook his
head, packed up his tools and was gone.

When my dad came home from the store, Mom, mad
almost to crying, just said, "I wish you'd look." And my dad

stepped out onto the flimsy new porch and cussed, though he always tried not to in front of me.

"Well?" she said when he came back in the kitchen.

"I didn't think he was that bad off."

"Ha. Everybody knows it. Even Dingle (who was the moron who spent his days crouched in the post office lobby) knows it. You didn't pay him, I hope." My dad just nodded. Mom said she guessed there wouldn't be much point in trying to get him up here to make it right for the next couple weeks.

My dad still looked out for Weasel's daddy, though. Even when he took to sitting in the alley all day dozing and drinking, Dad would slip out and give him a stale cake or fruit that was too bad to sell but you could still eat by cutting the rotten spots off with your knife. Sometimes he sent me. "Here, run this out to your buddy's daddy in the alley," and I knew who he meant. Weasel's daddy always took it but he never spoke, not even to thank me.

I was in high school by then and, yes, Weasel and I had gotten to be buddies again. This time it took a little better. We went out for basketball like about half the other boys in the ninth grade, each with our own reasons. We still bristled around each other but only halfway remembered the reason why. Still, when after three days of nothing but drills, the coach paired us all off to play one-on-one and Weasel and I got matched up, we both saw it as a chance to even the score. Weasel was a year older, quicker and had more basketball smarts, but I was taller and had learned a little how to use it. Because we were pretty even, the game got rougher and rougher. Both of us hit the floor a couple of times and only the coach sitting there smoking his cigar kept us from fighting again right then. We knew if we did, he'd throw us both out. When he blew the whistle and put some others out there, we had beat it all out of ourselves and went on over and sat in the bleachers together. The coach came by and said, "I want to see you both back here Monday," like it didn't matter one way or another to him. Weasel and I saw how we could be useful to each other.

That began my long and gawky apprenticeship in basketball. But Weasel already knew the game. It was in his genes; his body told him where to go and he went. Even with his skills, he was different than me, or any of the rest of us, for that matter. All of us wanted to win—after you lost a game and the coach raised hell with you and ran you like that, nobody would want to ever lose another one if he could help it—Weasel, though, was driven. Whenever losing seemed inevitable, he would go into a terrible fury of running and shooting and passing, demanding with his looks that we stick with him. And when his skills failed him, he used his elbows and fists. When we lost, Weasel took his revenge on the locker room walls, then went silent. But that coach knew how to turn Weasel's hungry meanness into grace and cunning.

We had some success and my dad was proud of me. He came to every game, even to Whitewood and Hurley way down in Buchanan County. Of course Weasel's daddy never quite made it. He was sleeping a lot by then; sometimes he'd just wrap up in his coat and sleep the night away right in the alley. My dad got so he was being dad to both of us, seeing to it that Weasel got the right things to eat and had a couple of good white shirts for the road trips. He slipped things into Weasel's mother's grocery sack, she being too timid to turn them down. When we stopped in the store on game days, Dad had ground steaks and hamburgers already made into patties for us both to take home and cook. Mom wasn't taken in. She'd always known where the Winstons Weasel was buying since he was eleven or twelve for his dad went; Weasel's daddy smoked nothing but Luckies.

No good could come out of my hanging around with that boy, she thought. And when Weasel started fixing the Mercury, she worried even more. Wasn't it natural, though, that he would take up the tools his daddy had left lying and take on that car just waiting to be driven again? When he started, he couldn't even drive, but he had the mechanical knack and pretty soon the car fired. Then he went to the body where there wasn't much point in trying to save the faded paint. Still he waxed it right off then took the Bondo and spray paint to it. On his birthday, Weasel hired the bootleg taxi and used it to pass his driver's test, thumbed to Tazewell and paid the higher price for tags without insurance. What money he couldn't get from bets and hustling—sure he bet · on us and only his pride must have kept him from betting against us sometimes—he took away from his mother. They lived on welfare then. As soon as he got home, he went for a ride. Dad and I picked him up in Big Vein where his radiator hose busted. All the belts, hoses, tires and gaskets were dry rotted but Weasel hadn't found them out in his sneak drives around the block. That first day wasn't the only time we picked him up except for the ball joints and shocks. But he finally got that Merc road worthy for our local orbits.

My mom called it an eyesore. For me, cruising with the Weasel at high speed, the car floating all over our lane and the next, sliding through the curves and bouncing down the hills until we pulled in behind the gym in a gravelly plash was the edge that I could take right out on the ball floor with me. Mom had probably called it an eyesore when it was new, I thought.

She said I was changing for the worse, too. Dad took up for me and she said she knew for a fact he hadn't hung around with the likes of that, meaning Weasel, when he was my age.

When the picture turned up, it proved her wrong. People were always bringing things in our store. It was kind of a town forum where people came to talk and leave off packages for each other as much as to buy their groceries. Somebody brought the picture in just for showing around. "See anybody you know?" Mom asked. I did, I saw the Weasel's daddy right in the middle of the back row of old time football players with their chaws and crazy leather headgear. He had his head cocked, hands on hips and, while the rest of the guys wore their helmets, Weasel's daddy's dangled off his wrist. He looked like he could whip the world; he looked like his son. "No," my mom said, "there." And in the front row, on one knee, looking away from the camera, was my dad, a humble soldier of the line.

"What was he like?" I asked my dad.

"Mean." Then he told how at Wytheville somebody tackled him and he swallowed his plug. A few downs later, he got tackled again and threw it up all over the guy who had him. The rest of the day nobody would touch him. "We didn't have any business winning that game, but we did." Dad smiled at me, and I felt like we were sharing a secret from Mom.

"What happened?" What happened so that people were now saying around that he had the shakes so bad he had to get somebody to light his cigarettes for him?

"He thought the world owed him a living, that's what," Mom told me.

"No," said my dad.

"What was it then?"

"Too proud," and he wouldn't say anything else. So when Mom said it was all the same thing, his silence said it wasn't but left me to figure out the difference.

What I had heard about him having the shakes was true. They said he had the DTs, too, and even shit blood in his britches before they got together by the pop cooler in the front of the store and decided what to do about Weasel's daddy. My dad took him. With another man, he bundled Weasel's daddy up in the old stadium blanket we kept in the back of the station wagon for emergencies and drove him to the VA hospital in Salem. "I don't care if he ruins the blanket," Mom said, "but I hope he doesn't die in the car." "He's not going to die," my dad said.

Weasel's daddy didn't die in the car that day; he made it until spring. The season was over, except it was never really over at Powell's Bottom. There were pick-up games every day after school and we were expected to be there. These were my favorite times, because there wasn't any pressure. Weasel hated them for the same reason, but he came. He came even if he laid out of school that day or was on suspension. Or got called out of class to the principal's office and disappeared as he had today. But Weasel wasn't there. After some pretty sorry play, the coach called it off and put us in the bleachers. He told us Weasel's daddy was dead and that six of us including me would be pallbearers and the rest had damned well better be at the funeral.

Mom cooked half a ham for Weasel and his mom. I wore my Sunday clothes and carried it with a couple of dish towels when we went to the house where the body was, since they couldn't afford the funeral home. Everything in Weasel's house was worn out but scrubbed clean and covered up with doilies in an embarrassed try to make up for it. Almost everybody from town was there, so that you could hardly get into the little front room where Weasel's daddy was in his coffin with two bowl shaped lamps at his head and feet and flowers crowded around him, more flowers than you might have expected for a drunk. Weasel's mother sat on the couch with a woman on either side of her, dried up and empty. Even with all her superstitious talk about ghosts, so that one woman had to stay over with her as long as the body was in the house and a few days after, I think she must have been relieved.

Some neighbor lady came and took the ham off my hands, and then my parents and I went up to look in at Weasel's daddy. I wanted to see if the dagger was still there, to see if maybe it hadn't just withered away. But the undertaker had crossed Weasel's daddy's hands in such a way that you couldn't see. And he'd fixed him in other ways, too, so he was small and waxy in his old double breasted blue suit, looking like the appliance salesman up at Montgomery Wards. Nobody bothered to claim he looked just like himself. Maybe they were just as glad.

But they weren't. After Mom went to the women in the dining room, Dad and I went to the men out in the yard. There it was all cigarette smoke and stories of Weasel's daddy. The Mercury and the swallowed tobacco of course, but more that I had never heard: Weasel's daddy in the Service, in the pool room, in school, in Pigg's garage. Everybody laughed big healthy laughs, then got quiet and sighed. They still loved him, but in these stories he wasn't the one I took the rotten fruit to in the alley. I stood by my dad and listened; I wanted to hear it all, even about him making me walk the bridge when they came to that. But the coach saw me and came up to me. I was the only player there; the rest probably thought the funeral was enough death to put up with, even for Weasel. Coach said, "He's out on the back step, go on back there."

I went around the wooden walkway past the tool shed and found him sitting just outside the square of light from the kitchen window, not even bothering to palm his cigarette. "Go in and get you something to eat," he told me.

I did and found the little enameled tabletop packed with all kinds of good stuff, cakes and cookies mostly, but the ham was there and some other meat plates. I cut off a big hunk of yellow cake and went back out. "You got enough in there to last a month," I said. Weasel didn't say anything, just sat and smoked. After a while he said, "Shit," in a way that made me lose my taste for the cake. So we just sat for a while and watched the butts that Weasel had flicked out into the yard burn away.

"Want to ride up Bluefield and pick up Debbie? She's off at eleven."

"I guess I could do that," I told him, sure my dad would let me even on a school night.

We pulled out from the house nice and easy, but once Weasel came out of the curve up the grade by the cemetery, he goosed the Merc, holding it in low range than knocking it into drive, squealing and laying a small patch of rubber. They could see us from Weasel's front yard, and I wondered if they, my dad and the rest of those men, were grinning at that moment and shaking their heads, whether they were saying that Weasel had a lot of the old man in him.

When we got to Bluefield, we bought a pint of Yukon Jack at the drive-through window of the West Virginia side liquor store where they never bothered to card you. Weasel told me to crack it open and have a drink. I took a small one and passed it to him. He took a healthy slug and then another one or two while we drove around waiting for the time to go to the country club where Debbie waitressed.

The clubhouse was up on a hill, up a little road you had to know was there to keep from missing. Except for a few cars in the parking lot, it seemed as lonely as the moon up

86

there. We went right up to the main entrance and let ourselves in. The dining room was empty but in a little alcove these men, some in golf clothes, some in business clothes, were playing poker. They looked at us like, what the hell, and I would have just as soon slipped back out the door, but Weasel held his ground and gave them the once over, too. Then we started for the swinging doors of the kitchen. "Next time go around back," one of the men said, too late.

Inside, the cook, another waitress and Debbie sat around, impatient and bored. "I told you not to come in that way," she said. Weasel just looked at her.

"Go on honey, we can close up," the other waitress said. "Sorry about your daddy," she said to Weasel. He told her he was, too. "Go on. They'll be here all night, you don't need to stay."

We all got in front and Weasel gave Debbie what was left of the pint. She wouldn't drink any, so he said, "Hold it then." Then we started up and Weasel drove to the end of the parking lot where he walked the big Mercury over the curb and we went off down the hill toward the practice green. Then, no lights on, we went skidding and sliding down the hill past the first tee and on to the fairway where Weasel gunned it for all it was worth and then locked the brakes. And so we went, the Weasel leaving his autograph in a long twisting script that covered most of the golf course.

We bumped over the ditch and out onto the main road where Weasel opened the door and looked under, "Nothing dragging," and went on. It wasn't until the light by the N&W underpass that I could hear Debbie sniffling and doing her best not to cry. Weasel told her to shut up, took the whiskey and finished the rest of it on the way home, driving too hard for any talking. We had to shut up and concentrate with him. When we pulled up in front of her house, they both got out on his side and Debbie wouldn't kiss him. "How am I supposed to go to work tomorrow?" She was crying.

"Oh hell. What makes you think they'll blame it on you?" he told her and stood there watching her into the house.

We went on to my house without talking. Then when we pulled up in front, he said, "You know why I had to do that."

I took out a stick of Dentyne to chew on before I went in and watched Weasel's taillights down the hill and out of sight. Yeah, I thought I did.

Roland Barker and his Red Guitar

"Well, I used to be a good cow hand, but things happen."
—The Ringo Kid
Stagecoach

Two days before our class reunion, Roland Barker tried to kill himself and mostly succeeded.

About the same time, I'm batting it across western Tennessee on my way home from Fayetteville, Arkansas. I like the trip, a thousand miles, fortify myself with a dozen oranges and a six-pack of Cokes, and lash myself to the wheel. Life on the Interstate Highway System becomes more pleasant after dark. Then it's me and WNO, The Truckers' Friend, playing more ballads of eighteen-wheelers than the average station wagon driver might care to know exist, at a tempo that can lock you into a steady sixty-five if you're keeping time by the seams in the pavement. Miles go by in clumps of ten and twenty, time in the half hours marked by wire service news headlines.

I pull off at a self-serve in Nashville, where the attendant is sitting on the pump island, shooting down moths with a water hose. Another guy is slumped over a pump, talking at him: "Going to Louisville, want to ride along?"

"Can't, got to work." They both laugh about this.

"Want me to bring you anything back?"

"Yeah, some pussy."

"Got to get some for me first," he says and slides off the pump, walks cowpoke style to a sixty-four Merc painted in one of those crazy Mercury Division shades, sort of a salmon pink, rakishly angled on the edge of the concrete apron. The attendant and I smile at each other when he starts it up. It's got a clean baritone rumble, dual glass packs on a solid V-eight, a strong, steady road car. He gives us a honk on the horn, roars off and up the access ramp, his tail lights disappearing at the same angle of attack as a carrier jet.

"Crazy bastard'll be there in two hours," the attendant tells me, "be back by morning." He doesn't expect me to be suprised. There are legions of crazies running up the highways every night. I, with my bug-shot windshield, gassing up and adding oil, halfway home at one-thirty in the morning, look to be one of them.

My dad calls me up from the store at four in the afternoon. The phone rings twelve times before I answer it. "I didn't wake you up?" he says.

"No."

There's a short conversation, the kind we usually have long distance, about business at the store, still in its steady state of decline, about goings on around town, mostly centered on the sick and dying since Powell's Bottom has its share of each. "Oh," he says just before he hangs up, "your buddy Barker drank some antifreeze, they say."

Is Roland Barker my buddy? I have to admit he is, but I never planned it that way. He's just a stray dog kind of guy, and I happened to be the one he took up with.

Roland Barker was not one of the people I'd thought about seeing at a reunion. In fact, I could go for long periods of time without thinking of him at all, and then he would just turn up, standing on the highway with a guitar in a sack, thumbing. And I'd pick him up. It's kind of appropriate, I think, Roland fits into my thoughts just like he had into our class. He didn't sit in the back of the room with the tough guys, the ones who disappeared a day after their sixteenth birthday, but on the side along the wall with the timid and dumb, the ones that get described in the teacher's lounge as just being there. I was one of the few who knew him well enough to know his middle name was David and that's what he preferred. But his teachers never caught on, his school name was always Roland.

I, on the other hand, was in the first desk of the front row, sprawled out in my varsity jacket, captain of the team and most likely to succeed. Every now and then when the teacher had somebody squirming over an answer to a question from an assignment that nobody'd bothered to read, I'd pivot around and look back at the class—a diamond with me at the point.

I found my senior year annual on the bookshelf and took it down. I'd planned to look through it sometime before the reunion anyway. There was Roland Barker in his teal blue tux jacket (all us boys got to wear one so we'd match; the girls were draped) and very slim bow tie, hunched over as usual, wearing an expression of deep concentration. It was the kind of look that must have made the new teachers think he must be thinking very hard about the answer to the question, so they called on him a lot. He never said a word, just shook his head and fidgeted. After a while, the teachers gave up, but he passed his courses anyhow. I can see now that what all his teachers took for concentration was one long eyebrow that needed plucking where it knitted up on the bridge of his nose. The thing is that back then when the biggest worry most of us had to think about was the old man figuring out somebody was cadging his cigarettes, Roland Barker was way ahead of us. There he was flanked out on the long side of my diamond, drumming his pencil and squirming in his seat, sweating. What's he got to be so nervous about, I remember wondering.

He had blue eyes, which like the jackets, didn't show up in the black and white pictures, and big pimples that the studios always airbrush out. But I can see those pimples just as clearly as I could from my vantage point in U.S. history. They were the kind with big white heads and tiny black dots in the center. Roland used to come into our store every afternoon on his way home from school and buy a bottle of pop and some peanuts, stand around and talk to my mom about just anything. Then as soon as he went out the door, my mom would say, "Oooh, I'd love to get the pimples off that boy."

There was something I'd forgotten about our old yearbooks. Every senior had his name written in full and under it was the nickname he'd been tagged with. Mine was Hound Dog and the other guys on the basketball team had names like Puddin' Head, Weasel, the Pirate. But under Roland David Barker, it simply said, "Dave."

I put on my jeans, sticky and baggy from being pressed twenty hours between my ass and a cheap vinyl seat, some sneaks too long sockless and a T-shirt featuring a skull wearing a crown of roses and paddle on down the street to face the music. It's turned out to be a pretty day, that mist I seem to recall from the trip in (ETA eleven a.m.) has blown off and the air is a sharp cool seventy degrees, mountain weather, weather that makes you want to hike or run or play a little ball, things I haven't done in a long time. Which only goes to show that a sunny day can brighten up just about any place. The row of garages where my folks say the punks go and smoke their dope, and which are sliding into ruin anyhow, look picturesque. In fact, you could turn a bunch of idiots with Nikons loose in this town and they'd have a field day: nothing but a bunch of falling buildings and lined-faced black lungers.

And there, right on the bisector of Center Street, is the Powell's Bottom Market, not looking so grand itself, gray cast-iron front on the outside, inside mostly an aqua with soot you could write your name in that gets pretty much on everything in towns where they burn coal and mine coal, or at least used to. It's all my folks can do to keep the dirt off the groceries.

Walking along, I see a few people, most of them are Dad's customers. They look at me with their faces angled downward, giving me a suspicious eye. For them, I think, it's that they don't want to embarrass themselves by not remembering my name so much as that I'm my dad's son, and then what it is exactly that I do. That's OK, it's easy to forget. Like so many other social invalids my age, I'm a graduate student in English.

For the same reasons, I angle my face downward, too, knowing these folks but wishing my memory were defective in a more useful way. I can remember walking through their back doors with a box of groceries under my arm, the oilcloth tablecloths, the chicken salt and peppers, the black mammy napkin holders, the dogwood blossoms on the plate that covered the flue hole. I'm ashamed, to tell you the truth. Somebody might come up and ask me a question about *Vanity Fair*, or *Erewhon*, or even *David Copperfield* for Christ sake, and I don't know nothing but Kurt Vonnegut and a bunch of movies. The fact that nobody's going to put me on the spot in this town just makes the phoniness that much worse.

A sign on the swinging door featuring the Virginia Slims girl sitting in a skirt that barely covers her ass says, "Open." I keep my hands in my pockets and meet the door with my body. Dad's sitting on the counter; one of the loafers is leaning against the pop cooler, sucking on a Double Cola. The loafer gives me a nod, my dad a smile. Just now they're locked in philosophical considerations, I feel it in the air. It could be the resale value of a seventy-three Chevy Caprice or a Remington pump shotgun, but today it's Roland Barker they're talking about. "Let's ask the perfesser," Dad suggests, a deferential, almost oriental, dip in my direction.

"What's that?"

"We was just considering what a slug of that Prestone might do to your insides."

I scuff the toe of my shoe against the black concrete floor, like Trigger puzzling through a particularly tough addition, "Tear up your stomach?"

"Well, we figured that."

"And probably go to your kidneys, too."

"Your kidneys?" They consider this angle, eyes shining like they know I'm full of it, but tomorrow it will be peddled on the street for gospel, Roland Barker's laying in the hospital with his kidney's shot to hell.

"Still in school?" the loafer asks me.

I give him a nod.

He gives me a wink. "Nice work when you can get it." They can sense their own kind.

At dinner my mother says, "What are you going to do with yourself?" her face flushed with disappointment. It's my own fault, sitting and wondering how Roland Barker is facing his slow death by kidney failure, I've allowed the conversation to drift into dangerous waters, my graduate work, or more specifically, when that graduate work will have run its prescribed course and I will enter the work force. I have lied and told her, "A while."

I don't have a chance. Which is not to say the folks at the University of Arkansas haven't been accommodating. They sell me football tickets at student prices and give me a hand-ball court during faculty hours. I take movie courses (Did you know James Arness was "The Thing"?), also the ones where the prof shows his slides of Ireland, and the ones where you meet at somebody's house and bring your own. They even pay me to tell freshmen anything I want as long as I take roll and keep my pants on. So far, nobody's bothered to check. But in the dean's office, a Baby Ben with my name on it is slowly ticking down. Come spring, I'll have to pass the comp or get out, and no questions from "The Thing" will be on it.

"I don't know," I say, finally getting around to her question. Looking up into the gold ball in the middle of the Sears chandelier over the dining table, I see myself there, a freak with a pint-sized body and a large pear head. I begin to waggle my head, watching the changes I can make it assume, first the fat part of the pear is at top, then bottom. Mom watches, seeing her twenty-eight-year-old son turning into a drooling quadriplegic idiot.

"Where will you find a job?" She's mad now, not concerned like before.

"I don't know." Still looking, a massive forehead, a water head baby. "I think I want to live in a beer commercial. You know, be a cowboy or a lumberjack or a fireman or something like that. The kind of job where you can go out and bust your butt all day and feel like you've done something. Then you just walk down the road with all your buddies and go into the bar for a cold one."

She gets up and leaves the table. I hear her dragging herself up the stairs and shutting her bedroom door behind her. Dad looks at me, not really pissed, just tired.

For the first time we notice a baseball game is on TV, eased by seeing the players, stubby and round as baseball players tend to be. The fielders smooth the dirt in front of them, fiddle with the webbing in their gloves, spit. Don't they all have something they'd rather be doing? No, I guess not. For somebody out there, it's probably a relief. We keep watching even though it's two second division teams playing for what?

Then there's one of those classic screw-ups where three guys are converging on a short fly ball with a lot of arm waving and caps flying and the ball dropping in safely among them. It's funny. And I know without looking his way that my dad has the same smirk on his face as I do. We've always shared an appreciation for the botch and bungle.

"I'm going down the street," I tell him.

"You'll probably find Old Man Barker in Bunny's." He smiles his dropped fly ball smile.

Bunny, whose real name is Brenda—it says Brenda's on the window glass in crooked home lettering since somebody fell through the professional job—is the chief draw for her place. Among her customers, she's thought to be good looking, has big tits, wears a sweater, black stretch slacks and wedge bedroom slippers. She lost it in the face years ago, never smiles or talks, just opens your beer and stares out the window while she waits for her money. I order a Busch; she offers me a Pabst or a Bud.

At Bunny's, longnecks have never gone out of fashion. I wish I could say Bunny also had Hank Williams Sr. on the jukebox and the customers linked arms and sang along with "Your Cheatin' Heart." But this is Powell's Bottom's old man's bar. And with the exception of a couple of punks playing the bowling machine, that same bowling machine I knew when it used to be Posi's, everybody here sits by himself, drinking past caring and glad to be alone. Roland's old man isn't here; but thanks to the miracle of free association, Roland himself is. Maybe it's the jukebox with the bass turned all the way up so the joint throbs with a dull pulse that drags all of us down with it. Maybe it's just the soft red party lights that try to put a happy glow on the skulls drinking at the bar.

But mainly it's the bad music. Roland Barker's only notoriety was through his band, a band that got to be a fixture around our school. It never had a definite name, one month it might be the Headhunters, another it was the Viceroys. I know that band must have come together when we were sophomores and just seemed to have been around forever because the songs never changed much, and except for Roland, the group never improved. So whenever the student council got around to planning each of the four or five dances we had every year, somebody always made the motion that one of the bands from Bluefield be considered, the Blue Chords who arrived in a metal-flake made-over Trailways, or the Collegiates who had a hearse. But when it got down to voting, there was no getting around it, Roland's band was all we could afford. A day or two after the posters went up, everybody knew the mysterious Pagans were just another incarnation of Roland's band. But we all went and danced to "Stagger Lee" and "Johnny B. Goode," out of fashion but memorable and easy to play.

The band had four members and an occasional extra, usually a lost soul honking around on the sax. Darnell was the bass player. At six-two, one hundred and thirty pounds, he suffered through each performance like a saint off a medieval altar piece. His only virtue was that he had the reach for his instrument. He wasn't particularly smooth though, preferring to change notes only when the chord changed. I can see his arm, no thicker than the neck of his guitar, his bony knuckly hand moving up the frets like something out of "Invasion of the Saucer Men." A guy I can remember only as Pecker played rhythm guitar. This Pecker had red hair and a slight stutter; it was a sport among my buddies to make him blush. On the bandstand, that was his perpetual state. Pecker knew more notes than Darnell, but he didn't have rhythm, and Roland spent his time adjusting the volume on his amp trying to cover Pecker's mistakes. Mainly because he had a little more money than the others, Randy was the drummer. His dad had bought him a Ludwig concert snare to play in the school concert band, but because he was only a freshman at the time, the big guys took over his drum and made him play cymbals. So he joined Roland's band and his dad bought him a trap set. Randy may have had some talent, but he was too good looking to practice. Girls went up to him during the breaks no matter what the band sounded like.

And there was Roland. As a guitarist, he was quite good by our contemporary standards. He could play the hard parts on "Pipeline," play the tough instrumental versions of "Louie, Louie," and "Walk, Don't Run" and make them come out like the Ventures did it. But he couldn't sing, and I always wished somebody would've told him to stop trying. He couldn't even handle "The House of the Rising Sun" where all you had to do was growl into the mike and cover it up with low notes on the guitar. His only memorable vocal was on "Wooly Bully," where in imitation of Sam the Sham he would sort of screech, "Watch it now, watch it!" Then everybody swore he sounded just like Sam.

When most people around school talked about Roland Barker's band, they didn't say so much about what they sounded like; it was what he looked like. His almost bottomless eyes seemed to be focused on nobody and on everybody at once like a cheap picture of Jesus. He hunched over his guitar, holding it close to his belly and kept his picking hand right down there by the pickups so that you got the feeling something secret was going on—just between him and the guitar. White froth gathered in the corners of his mouth, sweat popped out of his face. And even from the back of the room, I could see the wet stains in the pits of his sport coat. Watching him was like what happened to me a couple of years later in college when I walked in on a couple of my friends fucking. I'd never stopped to think how it looked to see two humans humping away. It made me embarrassed for me, then them, and finally for the whole human race. What everybody wanted to know was, did Roland Barker have to show himself like that to play his guitar?

I watch a game or two of bowling. This game's a long affair with a tin alley painted to look like wood. You knock down, or knock them up really, the two-dimensional pins by sliding this steel puck across the wires sticking out of the lane. The pins hover about two inches off the surface, a mystic's vision of bowling. There's a trick to the game, a trick that's been lost in the playing to this generation of players. By glancing the puck off the side of the machine, you can hit the wires at a forty-five-degree angle and get strikes almost every time. The punks are playing for quarters; I get in the game and take a dollar off the two of them. Because I seem to be an adult, they look at me, forlorn and shaggy, hoping I'll give them their money back and turn it into a learning experience. I pick the quarters off the machine, stack them, and shake them around in my fist as I walk out the door.

When he calls me Dog, I know it's Weasel. His hand comes out of the dark inside the van, parked along Center Street for months now I'm sure, waiting for something to happen. He takes me by my shoulder and shakes me a little as his way of getting back on familiar terms, and I remember that, unlike me, all his strength is in his arms and hands. His personality is there, too, hands that find their own way over any kind of metal or wood—girls too for that matter. He was the one who threw the passes, snaked them inside around and between two or three guys, threw them on the fast break, the kind of lead passes that bounce up from the backspin and wait for you to come get them. Clever too, the Weasel, knowing when to take the shot, when to be there when I needed him, me being doubled up in the post and him sneaking down the baseline on the offside.

"Same Dog," he tells me, making it serve as a compliment and a joke on me at the same time. At bottom he is cruel, like Mercutio or a Richard Widmark character with a sense of humor. When things built to a fight, I would see it coming from when he elbowed some dopey innocent in the belly or let a "son of a bitch" slide into his ear under the noise of the crowd and the floor, as slick as the passes. It was Weasel who tied Roland Barker up, and I was the one who let him go. Listening to Weasel talk as we got through the requisite, "How you beens?" and, "What you doings?" I can tell that he, too, probably not being able to put his finger on exactly the sore spot, remembers that something happened back in school and we haven't been pals of the first magnitude since.

I always went to the gym during my study period. Bastketball players got to go to the gym and shoot around during study hall, but I went there to get away from the librarian and did my studying in the score box that hung from the wall like a crow's-nest. When I climbed the ladder and looked over the side, there sat Roland Barker all bound up and gagged like a mummy, with tape out of a medicine kit.

"Damn," I told Roland, "Coach would shit if he saw all that wasted tape." He was mute and stiff as a tar baby, and I went on over and cut him loose from the folding chair with my knife, leaving it to him to pull the tape out of his hair. Tears came up from his eyes, and I pretended not to look curious to see the pain and still not have any part of it.

"So what's happening?" Roland Barker said, coming on casual once he got the tape off his face.

I was suprised when he didn't scurry out of the box as fast as he could. "Why are you here?"

He laughed and shrugged. "Here," he said and reached into his pants pocket and pulled out a little plastic peep show that showed color transparencies of several different naked girls as you pushed a button. Roland Barker always had that sort of junk, wire puzzles, trick card decks, fancy knives that his parents gave him—and bigger things, too, like a ten-speed bike back when the rest of us had only seen them on the back of comic books. They got him the guitars, too, later on. As a kid, I couldn't understand that, since the Barkers were one of the charity families at Christmas time. Right then, Roland was wearing a pair of cheap pointy-toed loafers with little silver stilettos on the sides where buckles might have been. But they were scuffed and split out at the arches. And I can only remember him having two faded paisley shirts, a green and gold one and a red and black one, both washed nearly to rags.

I looked at the first girl. She had nipples big as silver dollars. "You can have it," he said.

"Why?"

"You got me loose."

"So? Somebody would have got you loose sooner or later." I looked over at him, and he had a silly half smile on his face. Then I realized that after having gotten the tape off and getting through what should have been the worst of it, he was going to cry. And sure enough, a big old tear came out and went off his down turned face to the shiny varnished sea of the gym floor below.

"This is a suck ass place, you know that? A real sucky place." There wasn't much I could say to that. I just let him go ahead and sniffle and sob until he got settled down and gave his nose a honk. "You guys are bastards."

"Who?"

"You basketball guys."

"Maybe so." Roland Barker wasn't the first guy my pals had tricked up for one reason or another like being queer, or queer bait, or being too smart, or being too small, too slow, too shy. They got Roland Barker for playing his guitar, though I doubt if they knew that themselves. When you saw him play, you couldn't look away. And when he came off the bandstand, he'd be stinking and trembling. Whatever Roland

Barker was doing to himself up there couldn't be allowed to go on.

I flipped to the next picture, a girl looking at me over her shoulder with her butt pushed out toward me, not so good.

"Did you see the one with the tits?"

"Yeah, pretty nice. Where'd you get this thing?"

"I bought it when our band had a gig down in Bristol." That was a lie, but I let him talk. Maybe he would say something I could tell on him at practice.

"Listen: They got topless waitresses down there. One of them put her titties right in my face. I could have bit one."

"You playing your 'professional capacity' down there, Barker?"

"Professional capacity?" he said, forgetting for a minute his own words, him telling the president of the student council his band normally got eighty dollars a night in its professional capacity, playing for a school dance being an act of good citizenship and Christian charity. "Yes, hell yes. Eighty dollars a night, but we plan to go up once we get better known down there. The manager, he came up to me on the last night—we played three nights down there—and says, 'You boys are about the best we've had.' He's going to call around for us. We're going to be playing all over Tennessee, maybe even Nashville."

I slid the viewer back to him. "You can keep it," he said. I flipped my legs over the side of the score box and started down the ladder. "Hey, you aren't going to say anything?" I shrugged and went on down the ladder and out the door.

When I went to the dressing room after school, they were all talking about it, Weasel taking the lead and the credit. It had been a hell of a job getting Barker up that ladder without dropping him, everybody thought, funny as hell too. I just went on and got my stuff out of the drying room and started dressing. How Roland Barker had got himself loose was still a mystery, it seemed. Then Weasel looked over at me lacing up my Cons and knew: "Dog did it." "Sure," everybody said, "Sure it was Dog because he's always going up there reading a book or something." "Why'd you do it, Doggie?" Weasel put

101

it to me, and everybody else was stone quiet, expecting me to crack one like I usually did.

But it came out with just the wrong sound, and not meant to be funny at all. "I thought he'd been up there long enough, I guess," realizing it was a good way to open up a fight.

Weasel didn't come at me, just said, "Well, God damn you then," and went on out to warm up. The fine tolerance that good basketball teams are tuned to was lost right there. Afterwards, when passes were long or somebody lost his man, we didn't pick each other up, just bitched about it.

Weasel's van is painted up in a stars, stripes and bars motif with a cameo on each door of a cartoon weasel drawn after the bad guy animals in Disney comics. The long nose, the sly grin, the little trailing drool drop of lust capture the Weasel in the driver's seat well enough. "Get in," Weasel says, "Let's ride. Some kind of rig," he says when I get into my crushed velvet chair. "It swivels," meaning the chair. Everything inside is red, white and blue, too, including the windshield (blue tint) and the Playmate cooler on the floor between us.

He cranks the engine and pops in an eight-track, then with the dull blare of Aerosmith pouring out of the windows, we do the town in low range. The narrow coal camp streets, laid out when the miners who lived along them walked to work and it looked like they always would, are packed up on both sides with early '70s Chevelles and Plymouths muscled up with cheap chromed wheels from Western Auto, Hyjackers and Thrush pipes, any kind of junk that gets you a decal to go in the window.

It puts me in the mind of a B war flick. We're the nasty Krauts driving around in our speaker truck, "People of Cul-de-sac, it is futile to resist us." The old folks go blank and stoney when we pass, don't respond to Weasel's waves and nods. They go to sleep at night expecting to have their heads bashed, pocket money and old coins swiped.

Weasel doesn't speak, just points lazily with his Marlboro. And still trained to follow his subtle directions, I look to see the cars, chained coon dogs, young girls that Weasel thinks should interest me. We're doing the town as Weasel does it ten times a night. Sometimes Weasel salutes other drivers with his three-tone horn and they return friendly obscenities. Soon we'll park it down by the old Dairy Bar (used-to-be train station), closed up now with its back burned out. People get out of their cars and talk here when the weather's good like tonight, then after a while they do the town again and wind up back along Center Street.

Weasel is backing up on the school house hill, last stop of scenic interest before coasting to the Dairy Bar. The old school, my folks' high school, my grade school, has gone to hell—windows busted just for grins, ceilings coming down. Up in the woods beyond it was sort of a walk-up make-out place. Remember the rubber tree, I want to ask Weasel, which was what we used to call it because at least once somebody claimed his score by hanging a rubber off the tip of the tree limb. Nostalgia is not the Weasel's métier.

A new-model station wagon pulls up and cuts Weasel off, and a girl about fifteen with these cutoffs short enough that the pockets are out the legs opens the door and bounces her ass over. She leans into the van, giving Weasel a good view, bums a smoke and then rolls her eyes around in ways that mean to ask Weasel who is this funny-looking guy he's with.

"It's Dog," Weasel says. "We used to be stars together." I wag my head in a dumb but friendly way.

Silence. Then, "Well, listen then, you got any smoke?"

Weasel smiles, "Why don't you find somebody for Dog here and we'll go up on the slate dump and party?"

"Diane?"

Weasel makes an aw-fuck face, then he turns to me, "Chubby, big tits though, and she'll do just about anything."

"Why don't you dump me off down on the parking lot, and I'll take it on home when I feel like it?"

Weasel looks out the windshield a good ten seconds to give me a chance to reconsider. "But does she put out? Does she, you know, fuck?" Once the crucial question for both of us. And here this kid is ready to crawl back on the shag carpet

103

with me—sight unseen—for a couple of joints or three or four Old Milwaukees. Who knows, we might mix and match, try all combinations. My nuts are shriveling; confronted with free pussy, I find it's not what I want. "OK," he says, "if that's how you feel."

Nothing much is said on the way to the Dairy Bar. Weasel wants to know when I'm headed out. I tell him, after the reunion, and he lies and says he doesn't know anything about it. "Come to it," I say. "I will," he says, and we split up on that phony note.

Outside the van, I'm from a distant planet. The crowd on the parking lot seems to know me; I hear my name, throw up a hand and push off, studying the cigarette butts and smashed cups in the roadway. I cross over to the side of the street where the bank is and look across to Pinkeye's place. Inside it's a pretty fast crowd. Roland Barker's old man would know better than to go in there now.

Back up the street, I stop by the store to listen to the compressors knocking, the belts squealing, hearing nothing but sensing the impending disaster of melted ice cream and chicken pot pie. My dad, though, standing at these same double doors, could cut through the chaos and touch base with the walk-in, the frozen food, ice cream, dairy and produce cases—call up the wobbly pullies steadied and tuned by slats off the chicken crates, always expecting trouble but not afraid of it. Still, it tires him and makes me feel shitty for dragging Mom down and leaving him to try to fix it right. So I go into Bunny's to kill some time before going back to the house.

It's pretty still, but the lights are on. Dad's looking at the upstairs TV over the top of an old sports mag. I take a seat and watch enough to figure out that Ernest Borgnine and William Holden are down in this sub drinking black coffee and sweating through their khakis while some Japs in a destroyer up on the surface are following them around. Or maybe they are following, and somebody is running. Anyhow, somebody is following, and somebody is running.

"Did you find him?" Dad asks me.

"Who?"

"The Old Man."

"No."

II

There's no wake-up call for breakfast, just the furniture knockings that are old signs of hostility. I'd like to call it all off, apologize, except that we've never recognized verbal agreements in this family—some act of kindness, then, if I could think of one. But Mom escalates—she's thought it over and thinks I could do worse than be an over-educated Bartlett Tree Expert. Touché, Mom. I pause to appreciate her skills as a revisionist. Beginning with the glops of molten prose she would have poured on my head last night if she could have cut through her anger, she's reduced it to one well placed *mot*.

So much the worse because I get the message and the sadness that's behind it, too. Wouldn't it have been something if Sigmund Freud and James Clerk Maxwell could have gotten together? A little guilt demon, thus to drive our engines, might have been birthed. At this moment, I am so busy easing the world's energy needs I can't concentrate on the sports page.

We eat, listening to the clock grind its dusty gears until the phone rings with a bulletin from the front: Few customers, more bills, and, oh, Roland Barker has survived the night. With the help of an artificial kidney machine (I was right, how about that?), modern medicine has added another to the list of Roland's disappointments.

Mom suggests there's nothing much more sad and sinful than to take your own life unless it's maybe to take someone else's.

"Geeech," I say, ritually disemboweling myself with my knife fresh from the jelly.

After judging my shirt stained for good, Mom begins an elegiac account of the hard life and times of Roland Barker, with the subtext "Who knows what that boy could have amounted to if he'd had the chances you've had?" Amen.

Roland Barker, it seems, was born smack in the center of a seven-kid family, three girls ahead of him (I can scarcely remember any of them), two boys and another girl behind him to parents who never had a thought for anything more than taking whatever welfare, food stamps or commodities the state would give them and putting them towards beer at Bunny's when it used to be Posi's.

Mom used to stand up front by the window as the Barker parents passed our store on Saturday mornings and click her tongue at them. She didn't like them mainly because they would walk the streets, come in the store and buy a pack of L&Ms maybe and then go on home and phone in their order. My dad also carried them on credit. One day the Barkers caught my mom in a bad mood. They came in and were ambling up the aisles, not looking for anything in particular. Old Lady Barker was wearing this old, too long, blue skirt, pleated at one time, but just hanging now in a jagged hem. She always wore her hair up in a bun covered over with one of those gauzy scarves they sold at Kressge's And this morning she was making like a general out inspecting the troops, her skinny arms folded on her chest, clomping down hard on her heels, looking over our merchandise, "They got it cheaper at Kroger's, got more stuff, too." Old Man Barker dragged about a half a step behind her, and it looked like he ducked a little each time she said something.

Finally, they shuffled up to the checkout where I was standing, and she asked for her pack of L&Ms. I told her twenty-five and a penny tax and was sticking out my hand when she said, "Could you put that on the ticket? We're going to have a order today."

Before I could write anything down, my mom spoke up from behind me, over at the other checkout. "Do they put it on the ticket for you at Kroger's?"

"Mam?"

"You heard me. Charge a quarter's worth of goods. And I'll bet they deliver from up at Kroger's, too." Mrs. Barker pulled her head back, looked down her long nose, her nostrils

106

flaring like a horse's. She'd worked herself up to looking kind of dignified and aristocratic in a Colonial American sort of way. I just hung on to the charge book. My mom went on, talking to me now, "She can pay. She just wants to spend her pocket money up the street. On beer."

"Don't see where that's any of your concern," Mrs. Barker said, but she was whipped. Mr. Barker chewed his lip and kept his head down.

"And smoking cigarettes. In your condition. I wish you would look at those boys' shoes. How can you send them out to school dressed that way?"

Mrs. Barker was scratching around the bottom of her big white pocketbook, came up with a quarter and a penny and slapped them on the counter, "You don't need to come up that hill anymore, either." And they both walked out.

In the still aftermath, my dad said from the butcher shop, "You can forget about that thirty-five dollars they've got on the books."

I wanted to know what was Roland Barker's mother's condition. "Nothing that would interest you." But I went on and asked again, sensing Mom's powers to be at low voltage after that encounter. "Women's troubles. Things you couldn't understand at your age." It was something to do with sex then, and I knew it was pointless to ask anything more.

So Roland Barker's parents went shopping at the Company Store for a while. They even went to Kroger's when they could bum a ride to Bluefield. Some Saturdays I'd see them riding up the street sitting in the back of somebody's car acting like they were a couple of diplomats.

Roland never stopped coming to the store, though. Mom would take his stack of books and rifle through them for test papers, look over his report cards and tell him he could do better; and he'd tell her, "Yes Mam." The Mom, then and always trying to usher the world into a better age through sturdy and sensible clothing, hot breakfasts and a thorough knowledge of the states and capitals. She couldn't help seeing Roland for the raw material. "He's such a quick little boy. All his teachers say he could do, if only he would." She knew;

she'd taken Roland's case to each of them when they stopped in the store. And she made them agree with her despite their experience with plenty of others like him.

She even took up for him when the guitar business started, on summer evenings when Roland would flail away, still wrapped up in the noise of it. Everybody would be out on their porches, looking up the hill. People complained and threatened to call the cops, and my mom joined right in. Back in the house, though, she would say, "I hope playing that guitar makes that boy happy. It might be all the pleasure he gets."

"Well," Mom says, voice cracking, face flushed, as if it was her own son barely pulled back from the edge of death, "I think you ought to do something for him."

"Me?"

"You could make a speech for him at the reunion. You could get your classmates to pitch in some money to help pay his hospital bill. He's never had any regular sort of job, it's always been his music." There's no way out is there? I tell her I'll try to think of something, which is close enough to true to get me on the road to redemption. Mom offers to take care of my laundry needs; I thank her and tell her maybe I should get up to the Bluefield hospital to see Roland. I need to see him with the tubes coming out of his nose if I'm going to be his pitch man.

It's not like I haven't been here before. After the scorebox episode, Roland Barker watched me for a few days to see if I was going to blab. When I didn't, he got the feeling he could slip inside the force field I radiated, me being a hot jock, and breathe a little. And I felt it, too, so that I watched out for him in phys-ed and never let anybody throw his pants in the shower or spray Tufskin in his underwear. It wasn't that I was going to take up for him if it came to a showdown. I wasn't much of a fighter; I was the team diplomat, the one the coach sent out to apologize to the refs after technical fouls. If Roland Barker got his butt beat, it was his problem as far as I was concerned. But the guys respected me enough to lay off of him.

At the dances he got so he'd sidle up to where I was sitting in the back of the cafeteria with the rest of the unattached basketball players. He'd sit down and light up a cigarette, take a few long drags and exhale out his nose. We were buddies, and so I must understand his problem of being a great guitarist saddled with a trio of clowns. Actually, he didn't know how close he was to exceeding the bounds of my limited protection.

"How's it sound back here?"

"Real good," I'd say. I could feel the rest of the guys wanting to break loose, to just bust out laughing or grab him by the coat collar and drag him outside. They'd be saying, "Oh shit," and groaning. Roland would just go on smoking and keep his back to them.

"That damned Pecker. And Darnell," he'd say, meaning it for the rest of the guys more than me. "You've got to watch them every minute. They can't even get the chords down." Somebody behind me would make a farting noise; Roland would go right on. "Randy, at least Randy's got rhythm." I'd nod and he'd say something like, "How'd you like that new wah-wah pedal I got?"

He was always getting new equipment. "Tough," I'd tell him.

"No lie?"

"No, it sounds great. I kind of like the way you work that into 'Smoke Gets in Your Eyes'. It gives it a whole new sound."

"Hey," he would say, leaning in so I'd know this was the real inside scoop, "If I didn't have to play with those guys, you'd really hear something."

Sooner or later, somebody would start up a little chant like, "I'm going to kick a skinny little butt," and so on until Roland would grind out his cigarette and beat it back to the bandstand trying to act like he never heard a word.

"What's he want with you?" they all wanted to know.

"I don't know."

"Ah, you're queer bait, that's what it is." I had to take it for that little bastard.

Dad presides over his noisy realm with a cup of coffee, shoots the breeze with the various salesmen. Business is slow, they all agree; I can't remember when it wasn't. He reports Old Man Barker has been sighted, came in to charge some white bread and bologna and to mooch a box. Of course the Barkers came back to our store, sneaking in when Mom was out, broke and begging. My dad could overlook the dusty *No New Accounts* sign stuck up beside the cigarette rack; the Barkers already had an account. And they still owed on it and how else was he to get his money? he'd say when he and Mom argued about it over supper dishes. For a few months the Barkers made Dad look good, paid in full when the checks came, then it was back to their old ways.

By this time my mother must have decided that I was old enough to understand women's problems. She wrote me at college that Roland's mom was dying of cancer of the uterus but was firm in her conviction that her lungs and liver were shot, too. Anyhow, Roland thumbed all the way home from Fort Bragg on a weekend pass, and I happened to pick him up outside Blacksburg, standing there with an old acoustic guitar in a laundry bag, then piling in my car soaking wet like it happened every day.

They didn't even keep Roland's mother at the hospital in the end because it was too expensive and there wasn't anything the doctors could do for her, anyway. They had her lying on that old maroon sofa, the relations gathered around bawling and drinking and waiting. I think she hung on just to see Roland one last time. I like to think that Roland's mother loved him, father, too, for that matter. What else could you think when you saw all the rusty toys in the yard? But I remember her bringing Roland's little brothers to the store. They'd be whining and begging for ice cream or suckers. She'd tell them to shut up for a while then get sick of hearing it and give in. Then they'd be whining a few minutes later and she'd turn around and slap them.

When we got to Roland's house that night, he took me in for coffee but there wasn't any, so I stood around the corner a while and nobody noticed. Roland took out the guitar, sat down beside his mother and played "In the Sweet Bye and Bye" and "Mother's Not Dead, She's Only Sleeping" while an aunt who was in the choir up at the Pentecostal Church sang. Then his mother said, "I can die now. Somebody reach me my cigarettes."

Old Man Barker went on a drunk and took off for a couple of months after that, left another big bill at the store. When he showed back up in town again, he came dragging back to Dad. I guess he's been in and out of the doghouse several times since then.

"You give him the box?" I want to know. The social history of Powell's Bottom could be written around who my dad denied boxes to, who he gave them to, or who he actually saved them for.

"I told him to go in the back and see what he could find." It's mercy then. Old Man Barker, not in a state of grace, still gets to sift through boxes too little to be used for anything else. "His boy tried to kill himself," Dad tells whatever salesman this happened to be. A shame, they think.

I make haste. The Old Man will be, I guess, standing at the thumbing place down by the Ashland station. He is, Luck's Green Beans box under his arm, tricked out in kelly green jogging gear and Zips. My, haven't the new knit fabrics changed the face of poverty! The Old Man eases in, keeps the box on his lap and calls me mister, as in, "Where you headed, mister?"

God damn it, you fart, I want to tell him, you know who I am. How many pokes of Redman have I sold you? But no, let's do it his way: "Bluefield, you?"

"Bluefield. Downtown." All the while his eyes are dodging all over the countryside; my car with its original equipment shocks rolls on heavy emotional seas. Then finally he comes out with it, "Near the hospital."

"You got somebody there?" All innocent.

"Son," he heaves up and lets me have it: His boy is dying up there, has gone blind and does nothing but cry out like a crazy man all the time he's not doped up with medicine.

"What's his trouble?"

"Took poison. God only knows why." I'm inclined to agree, but go ahead and say, "It must have kicked pretty hard on the way down."

"It was a mistake, he was drunk. He didn't know what he was doing," Old Man Barker says, reversing his ground, trying to get out of this conversation where I, by putting my snot nose in, have violated the whole hitch-hiker—hitch-hikee relation, that dual confessional anonymity. He just sits and tears at the side of the box.

"What's he do, this boy of yours?"

He pouts for a while, looks out at another perfect summer day, trees in full foliage covering up the pitched beer cans and Pampers. It's a beauty outside luck or fairness, and it breaks the old man down to talking again, "Guitar, played guitar. That's what he lived for."

"He like his work?"

Old Man Barker looks blank, "I couldn't say."

I tell him I go to all the joints around Bluefield and suggest maybe I have heard his boy play. The old man shakes no. I list some clubs for him, "Red Barn? Sky Club? AmVets?"

"Them, he played them, others too. Places in Beckley, Roanoke. They say he was good. I couldn't say, no ear for it myself. But unlucky, gets it from his daddy." He allows a smile, that old country-western pride in being down and out.

"What's his band?"

"Davey Barker and his Country Playboys."

"And he was?"

"Davey." Of course. And I tell him now I can remember his boy, a small guy, played mean guitar. One dance, I say, I can remember very well:

We, Roland and I, worked together briefly after graduation in the coal company warehouse—rubber boots, fan belts, funny shaped tires and other junk. I stayed until time for college, Roland until he pulled the delivery truck in front of an oncoming Dodge. He was 1-A anyhow. Still, everybody there put up with him as long as he did his job. He had left his buddies Darnell, Pecker and Randy behind for another band, a real band in his words. We heard about it every day at lunch. And when Roland asked us to come hear him play, everybody said OK, but I knew if anybody showed up it would have to be me. I didn't much want to go either, but I did mainly to show the other guys they were being assholes.

It was an AmVets' dance all the way over in Red Ash, and my dad didn't much want me to go. It was, he thought, the kind of affair where you came out to find your tires cut and your hubcaps gone. I told him it was at the American Legion and it was Roland Barker and he gave in. He'd want to hear about it in the morning.

It was the kind of place, as it turned out, where you could get your tires cut, a long barn shape built up mostly from used cinder blocks, some painted bright green in their previous incarnation. One lonely mercury light was in the middle of the parking lot, made with fill dirt so that I left the car thinking it might be swallowed up before I got back to it. Inside, naked one-hundred-watt globes hung from the ceiling down to rafter level, crepe streamers, a low plywood bandstand against the back wall. At a couple of tables pushed together near the door I came in, AmVet ladies sold Pabst, RCs and Nehis out of tubs full of ice. I bought an orange and swigged it slow, found an open spot and leaned against the wall. I was feeling conspicuous, knowing nobody and not wanting to dance anyhow. As long as I had the soda, I had a reason for being. I'd make it last.

The crowd was mostly mid-twenties, early thirties, about that age when you figure out that top-forty isn't charting your life anymore. Hot cars and true love doesn't seem to fit, so switch it on over to country where life's lying and cheating, drinking, trouble at the workplace, and a generally tearful vale. Despite this terrible lyrical burden, folks were jumping, that is, up, and dancing every dance. Most of them were drunk enough to feel loose, dancing old-style, fox trotting maybe, or some dance like that where you're holding on to your partner and spinning her every now and then. On the slow ones, it was what they'd done in high school, hugging and necking around the floor. There were the stags, too, a couple of them hanging on the wall like me, some more back in the corners all pretty drunk and looking for some action. And there wasn't any that wasn't spoken for.

This guy with a moustache that gave him a Wyatt Earp look and wearing a Yankees ball cap came in and stood beside me. "Who's the band?" I shrugged because I didn't know. It was another Roland Barker band with a silly name that wouldn't sound right no matter how many times you heard it. I'm sure Roland told me. I probably forgot on purpose.

"Guy playing the guitar thinks he's hot shit."

I shrugged again adding a tilt to my head, indicating maybe so, but he still plays pretty good. The guy looked back at the band, and I noticed how he kept his hands barely in the back pockets of his jeans, no thumbs through the belt loops, just his finger tips in the pockets down to the first knuckle. That way if there was any trouble, he could get them out in front of him fast. I slid my Nehi bottle down my leg and set it against the wall. Empty anyway.

"I like the gal, though."

I decided to agree with him on that. She had on tight jeans and a pink sweater, shaking it a lot, blond beehive. When she sang, she sounded like a bleating sheep but on key, and that sheep bleat worked well enough on the weepy ones. She thought she was sexy and the audience seemed to agree. The rest of the band were four slow-handed gum chewers in checked shirts and bandanas. Still, they were probably better sidemen than any others Roland had ever played with. I saw that they didn't like him much. Before, there had probably been four of them and the girl. She could carry any melody as long as it was down tempo and then they could step out for their unimaginative solos.

They were still doing mostly hillbilly oldies, but Roland had pushed the tempo up to something between Bob Wills swing and rockabilly. His guitar licks were full of sneaky references to Buddy Holly, Chuck Berry, Eric Clapton even, getting about as far from that tub thumping bunch behind him as he thought the audience could stand and then pulling it back in with a little Chet Atkins flourish to let them know it was country all along, just a little on the wild side.

114

Nobody seemed to mind, in fact they kind of liked the sound. Except for the crowd in the back corners. I could sense a hostility building the way you can when you're beating a good team on its home floor and the people in the stands start thinking, "This ain't right." It was all focused at Roland, of course. Besides the way he always had of fondling the guitar like somebody's naked body, he'd turn to the girl singer during his solos like it was all meant for her.

The band played old stand bys: Hank, Tammy and Loretta, a little Merle and Johnny Cash, early and late Elvis. They closed the first set with "Walking after Midnight," the girl struggling to keep up on her vocals until Roland got behind her and pushed her with his guitar. Then he was running out in front of her melody, slipping up behind it, going over it, inside it until his solo break came. The petal steel guy acted like he wanted in, too, but Roland wouldn't break off—he wanted the guy to come on in and play against him for a while before he gave over. The petal steel tried, but Roland was all up and down the neck, fancy picking, too. Finally, the guy dropped out and just went along behind, echoing Roland and highlighting some of the licks he could follow. The girl came back in, and they finished out strong to lots of applause. Hard feelings, though, in the band as they broke apart and left out the side door.

I went up to the table and made it a beer this time. Just about then everybody made for the doors. By the time I pushed through the crowd, I'd gotten the gist of it. It was Roland and some guy over the girl singer. He looked like a defensive end or linebacker out of Richlands with maybe six or seven years with Island Creek Coal. There were some others on the side, lined up like they wanted to harmonize in a barber shop quartet. Wyatt Earp was with them.

"What's going on?" I said and nobody paid any attention. "I just want to make sure it's a fair fight and all of you don't jump on him."

"What makes you think they'd have to?" Somebody back in the crowd said, and everybody laughed, including me. Roland looked at me, already in pain, and I tried to give him a look that would say I'd gone about as far as I could in saving his ass without losing my own. I was resigned and even understood it. These guys, drunk, horny and pissed off at nothing so much as a long run of rotten times could take a little of the edge off watching Roland get busted up in the parking lot.

The girl stood on one side, disgusted mostly. It was over pretty quick. The guy only hit Roland in the face once, but he went at him hard and steady in the body. Then, everybody went on back in, the girl walked around the back of the building and the defensive type followed her. The guy with the Yankees cap came over and flicked his lighter in Roland's face, "Dumbass." We put him in the back seat of Dad's car and I drove home fast, afraid all the way Roland would puke in his sleep and start to choke and I wouldn't be able to remember the first aid to save him.

By the time I punched it into second and got the car up the hill to the Barker house, Roland was awake enough to get up to the porch hanging on my arm. Old Man Barker met us at the door in his undershirt, fly down, cackling. He was always a happy drunk. "Some gal cause this?"

I called him sir. "Yes sir," trying to make sure he knew I didn't have any part in it.

"Regular tail chaser, this boy," he said with father's pride and dragged Roland in the house.

Backed into a corner, the old man remembers; he'd rather jump out of the car. He squirms around in his seat and I let him. Finally he comes at me, "Since you know my boy, mister, maybe you could drop by a minute and see if you can have any luck at cheering him." I'm only embarrassed at having gotten what I want so easily.

There's more. "He always was a fool for women," the old man says. Roland was married, she left him. If it wasn't the singer in the pink sweater, it might as well have been. He never figured to hear from her again after she went off with one of the members of his band to Buchanan County. Then she had papers served on him for non-support of two of the prettiest children you'll never get to see. And neither will Roland. Even with him dying, she calls him a bastard and won't come near Bluefield or Powell's Bottom either one. "She was a whore, still is one." And then, "He was a fool for it. I knew it was going to be that way when I caught him looking at a fuck book when he was twelve. 'You know what that is boy?' 'I know what it is,' he says, 'I'm just trying to figure out how you get it.' Ha. Ha. I told him right then, 'They'll get you in trouble, you best use a protection.' " He gets quiet, says, "They did, too. Women." Then quiet again, a practiced enough liar to know an excuse from an explanation.

Outside, the Bluefield Sanitarium looks like a hospital where Al Pacino would be watching over Brando as the Godfather. Inside, nobody seems to be too glad to see Old Man Barker and me. We're advised at the reception desk that it's family only in intensive care. "My other son," the old man says glossing over the foot height differential and the Gray Lady with the laser in her eye lets me pass.

The man knows his way, and from the few times I've been here with my own broken arm and tonsils and my kid pals' appendices and football injuries, I do, too. It's the same sanitarium, a dingier green with more of the plaster chipped. Old Man Barker, cowed almost to invisibility by the place, walks down the very edge of the hall on the black border, not the green and gray checks worn through to the concrete. The halls are empty, quiet except for the gurgles and moans that escape from the rooms over the sound of the rented TVs. Before the new hospitals in Richlands and Welch went in, they used to have the dying lined up out the doors. Old hillbillies would be in the hallways whimpering under their oxygen tents, figuring out by the hour that there were worse things to be than dead.

We get to the nurses' station up on the fourth floor; the day shift nurses cut their eyes at each other—they know the old man well enough by now. He goes straight for the room.

"Mr. Barker." Her nurse voice freezes Old Man Barker in mid-step. "The doctor is here; he'll see you."

He's a big bastard, this doctor, barrel chested and hairy, popping out of another room on cue. It's almost an ambush. He must be internal medicine; he couldn't be sticking those hairy arms down somebody's guts, could he? He looks at the little old man and me, all business—this is after all one of their charity cases. "To be brief," he says, fixing his eyes on me as the responsible party here. To be brief, Roland is a mighty fucked up boy. Seems his belly and throat are burned up, lungs too, even the lining that goes around his heart and lungs. Blind too, but here's the good news: The dialysis machine has, just like an old Taryton filter, charcoal and all, cleaned that antifreeze poison right out of Roland's blood. His sight will start to come back in a few days. As for the rest, just keep that IV plugged in and rely on the body's ability to heal itself. "He's got to want it, though, want to live." Right. Just like a fullback on third and three, Roland's got to hit that line. With his white corpuscles doing what they can, Roland can use his willpower to run to daylight. And now to the point: Roland's about due to be sent downstairs to one of the men's wards where he won't be crowding all the expensive equipment. He'll still have half a dozen tubes running in and out, but there won't be all this around-the-clock monitoring. Sure enough, over at the nurses' station are all these TVs beeping and pinging and making the jagged but regular lines of Roland's condition: critical but stable.

The doctor's off in a cloud of authority. The old man leads me to the room where Roland lies, eyes bandaged from the light, scrawny and shrunk to lumps for feet and his abdomen, pale head on two stiff pillows with not so much as a zit to give it some color. There's oxygen going into his nose and a suction hose in the corner of his mouth, but I see he can talk.

He's alert. "Who?" he says. But does he hear us or just sense us?

"Boy, I brung somebody to see you. He says you're buddies."

"Hey Barker."

Roland gets still with that special rigid concentration of the blind, and then says around the suction tube, "I know you but not your name."

Should I be suprised? "Dog," I say, "It's Dog."

"Dog!" He winces with a smile. "Dog, we had some crazy times, didn't we?"

"Sure Barker." The old man positively beams, that boy of his, loved women, loved a good time. We all sigh together.

"Well," I say, but let it go. How could I guess what crazy times exactly we were supposed to have had? So the old man and I shuffle around. He bites a chaw off his plug and offers it to me; I shake my head. "They don't mind it," he says, nodding toward the nurses' station.

"Daddy," Roland says, "I'm going to die."

"Don't talk that way. The doctor says you got to show your grit. He done his part and says you can make it."

Roland just shakes his head.

"Lord, lord," says the old man, easily resigned to what we can't understand.

"I was wanting to tell you before that I think you and Momma..."

"You'll be seeing her soon I reckon."

"Yep." He starts sobbing and kind of choking on the tube. The old man is crying, too. I step to the window. "You did the best you could by me. Us. All us kids."

"Maybe you ought to go on and die then." Ever the doting father.

I consider that maybe Roland and the old man are faithful to their version of Heaven—BarcaLoungers and color TV sets—not so much rest as relaxation, the good life that they and their kind feel gypped out of here on Earth. Old Lady Barker's there already, lighting her cigs on a five-pound table lighter of solid silver in the shape of a genie's lamp, laying back to watch her stories coming in with crystalline reception.

Roland says nothing for a while, then says, "Daddy, you still here?"

"Still."

"Daddy, I messed up. I know I'm going to die now. No matter what the doctor says. I got to. It's no point is there?" I look out to the ridge above the N&W rail yard at the Appalachian Power billboard where a neon electric motor still drives its little pulley. "I done my crying last night. For you and the rest of them," meaning his brothers and sisters. "And for the girls, especially the baby. I bet she's out of her diapers. Even her," the wife.

"That's good. You don't want to die with any hate in your heart. You don't want to die a sinner. Ain't it?" he says to me.

"No," I tell Roland.

"Daddy?" Roland starts again, "Daddy, you remember at Christmas that time I got my guitar? That little old red one with just one pick-up? How we took it home to Bluefield on the bus and you let me play it right then and not wait until Christmas Eve? I still remember how the sound came out of the amp and filled up the house. The very sound I remember. And when I'm just laying here all doped up, I can hear all the songs I used to play at one time or another, but it's not like you would hear them just whistling or playing by yourself. I can hear all the parts and they all sound good. I want to die like that." He's smiling and crying at the same time.

After a while, the sound levels out to his breathing with the suction, like walking across some swampy ground, and I realize that Roland has fallen asleep. I go up to the bed where the old man and I look on like a couple of stumped jackleg mechanics at Roland's bandaged face.

The old man follows me out into the hall, claws into my biceps with his yellow nails. It hurts, damn it. "Mister, you got to help my boy," he says.

"I will," I tell him. How else can I get my arm loose?

Outside, I push the button on my emergency brake— just like the trigger built into the joystick of a P-38, coast down the long hill in front of the cop station, throw it into second, pop the clutch and off I go in a cloud of my own.

I see Weasel's van pulled nose first in the Dairy Bar parking lot, pull in myself beside it. Weasel's around on the old loading platform, smoking dope, doesn't hear me come up. In the sunlight, his face is flabby, puffed, red-eyed. If he looks like hell now, what will another five years get him? "Weasel?"

"Shit. You scared me," he says and sticks the joint in my direction. "You missed it."

"I can see that."

"Well, hell, I just got up. Give me another hour and I'll be ready to rock and roll again."

"Coming to the reunion then?"

He stalls. "Dog, I don't know about you. Why you want to be running with those butt fuckers, I don't know." Maybe like Roland Barker, the Weasel is one of those from right around here that nobody tried too hard to locate even though he's still in the same house with his mother as when we were kids. "You go for me, OK?" He smiles.

I pull myself up on the platform and sit down. Weasel takes an empty pony bottle and starts throwing it over his shoulder and catching it behind his back. It's one of those Weasel tricks; he used to be able to do it forever, stone drunk, without missing.

"Hear about Barker?"

"Dumb fuck couldn't even kill himself right."

"I rode his old man up to Bluefield and went in to have a look at him."

"That's about like you." He sits the bottle down. "What was with you two, anyhow? He wouldn't have lived this long if you hadn't always been going around covering his ass. It was like you had ESP sometimes. Barker would be that close and here you'd come around the corner. Whoops, better not, Dog's his buddy and all that. Why? There were guys who said you were going queer on us and after last night, I might believe them."

Now, I smile. "Listen, I want you to do me a favor. I want you to go with me up to Bluefield tomorrow night and help me sneak Barker out of the hospital."

Weasel suggests I haven't gone queer, just crazy. I look over across the rusty railroad tracks and wait. "Seriously?"

121

"Seriously. He wants to die; they won't let him. We'll just go up there and carry him up to the Barker place so he can die on his own living room couch with a stack of Willie Nelson on the stereo."

Weasel shrugs to indicate that makes sense, but, "It's not so easy, see. There are those who'd like to see your buddy Weasel in jail. I don't know how much you know, but one fuck up like this one could be enough to get me there. So I'd like to help you out but..."

I scratch my head and suggest maybe I could offer some money to ease his nerves. How much and do I have it? No, but I think I can get it—a hundred dollars. Weasel is for it now. We shake, which is what I like about Anglo-Saxon hill stock: Offer them a little money and they'll lend their names to any cause, even claim to see the honor in it. We make a little plan and Weasel walks me around the building to my car and says, "Jesus God, Dog, is that your car?" It's an army green Datsun dented to hell, even on the roof, mismatched hubcaps, gas flap torn off, grill bashed. And you can't even see the worst, the battery held in with a piece of coat hanger, frayed belts and hoses, trunk cluttered with full water jugs and empty oil cans, a can opener stashed under the hood for convenience. I have a hood ornament though, a swan with light-up blue wings—something I picked up from J.C. Whitney's when I had nine-ninety-eight plus postage and handling that I thought I didn't need. It looks more like a goose than a swan. But I like it and turn it on with a little toggle under the dash when the mood hits me.

"Turn on the bird," Weasel says when I get in and crank it.

"Nah." I find the gear and am about to pull out when Weasel asks me, "You think Alice Ann will be there?"

"I don't know" I haven't seen her, haven't heard from her since graduation, which doesn't mean I haven't heard about her, thought about her.

"She's still married, you know."

"I figured she would be."

"You're stupid as Barker." This said kindly.

"You get any last night, really?"

"Titty, nothing but titty. A little hand in the pants, but what's that?" We shake our heads, it's the youth of today. As I drive off, I hear a bottle smashing over on the back side of the Dairy Bar.

Alice Ann, though, came to all the games. I remember her best standing with one tiny fist ground into her hip, glaring at the ref. Not a cheerleader, and past the ninth grade, never aspiring to be one, she found her true place in the knot of school-spirited girls who sat behind the cheerleaders, cheered the cheers with grave abandon and bit their nails and cared beyond reason regardless of the opponent or what the score had gotten to be.

When the crowd stood, she was always the last one down, fixing the refs with her brown bird eyes, secure in her knowledge that whatever the call, she was right. And she was. The only girl in those dark days who understood the rules— the subtle distinction between block and charge, the shooting versus the non-shooting fouls, even the traveling violations on inbounds plays—things some guys on the team didn't even know. How she learned the game, I never knew. She had no brothers; her dad worked hoot owl shift and drank all weekend, and I never recall seeing him on school property, not even for our graduation. For a while I had the idea that maybe she'd learned the game on account of me. But in that, as in so much else I attached to Alice Ann, I was mistaken.

We used to do our geometry homework together during first lunch period, we two and the hangers on who used to marvel at our genius as we ripped through the proofs. What nobody ever seemed to figure out was that all geometry takes is some memory and to be able to think in a straight line. But after we'd done the problems and passed the right answers around, Alice Ann would give me a critique of our last game. I was a great one for getting three fouls right off, usually for going over somebody's back or trying to block a shot, and having to watch most of the second quarter. In my estimation, I never committed a third of these fouls, and Alice Ann took my part. We were strong believers in what the TV color men call incidental contact. Anyhow, I took these generous critiques to be her shy way of coming on to me.

But she wasn't shy. Five-three and feisty as a bobcat, the kind who always saw the teacher's mistakes and couldn't let them go, always carrying her test paper up to the front and showing how she'd found her answer right in the book, intimidating her teachers into all-A report cards. Always in control, Alice Ann in her too longish skirts that never rode up and her blouses fully buttoned. And lovely to my eyes with her small low breasts and sharply defined leg muscles, with her glasses even—without them I was sure she would look quite Egyptian, one of those slight and dark eyed beauties shimmying along a pharoah's tomb. She was never thought much of by anybody else, though—no tits and all.

"Look at her," Weasel would tell me almost ready to break down and cry in despair, "A titless French horn-tooting cherry. And she's going to stay that way." And I would keep on looking, and Weasel, "I don't mean just church; I mean prayer meeting, too. You think you're going to get any off something like that?"

"No," I said with true conviction, knowing there was something in her worth going after even if I was too stupid to explain it.

"Come on, listen to Weasel. I know the ones who put out."

And there was the problem of Hobart, the one she'd gone with since before I'd ever known her in the eighth grade, she having gone up the valley to grade school. Hobart who wore his green Big Mac work pants and a white short-sleeved shirt and Goddamned black service shoes to school every day. Who was a true genius, not a fake one like me, or a worker like Alice Ann, a real math whiz who got to go to Virginia Tech in the summer for special brains math classes and came back with a foot-and-a-half-long Post VersaTrig slide rule which from then on he wore to school every day, too, dangling it from his belt like a sabre. Squinty Hobart with glasses coming down his nose, but the biggest knuckled—he took a size thirteen class ring—hand I'd ever seen.

They went to the same church, and it galled me to think about them sitting there side by side in that Baptist congregation—the very model of youth preachers are always hoping to find. She could have been with me, and I used to fantasize about it constantly. Some of the usual adolescent stuff of having at her in the back seat of the old Chevy, but these other fantasies, too, where we'd be in a home at big adult-looking desks where, papers stacked neat and squared away, we would be solving complex problems—beyond geometry into calculus even—together. Or maybe sitting close on a big couch, each plowing through a weighty tome when I would turn to her lovingly and make some impossibly brilliant comment on politics maybe, and she would smile and respond in kind, and that would be bliss.

I'd be sitting out behind the gym with Weasel when here they'd come in that boulder-shaped fifty-one Plymouth of Hobart's, Alice Ann sitting demurely close to him, up on the transmission hump but not touching, no smooches when they'd get out of the car and head into the building for some last-minute studying.

"Why don't you just fight him and then after you'd kicked his ass, you could claim her?" That was always Weasel's solution. But I imagined those ham fists and thought better of it. And besides, it might work for some gum popping twat that'd been plowed by half the class, but I knew it wouldn't work for Alice Ann. "Well, piss or get off the pot."

Right. So Hobart was two years ahead of us and went on off to Tech at last to be some kind of engineer. That's when Alice and I got to be big geometry buddies. And other things as well, such as when Hobart couldn't make it home for the weekend, Alice Ann would come to the after-the-game dances with the other pep types and I would be over in the other corner with the players. Everybody would be bugging me about her: Would she like a soda maybe? Why didn't I just mosey over her way? When was I going to ask her? And I swear it took all my nerve, even for a fast dance. I had asked for a slow one only once and knew enough not to ask again. Finally, Weasel and I cooked up this betting system where everybody would bet on which fast dance I would ask her. Sometimes we'd rig it which helped get me into action.

Anyway, I got the idea she liked me, as we used to say, and that maybe she was just waiting for me to give a little tug, and she'd come loose from Hobart with whom she'd steadied for five years already. Based on what? Well, there was her enthusiasm for my basketball play, for one thing, and the radiant and fulfilled look she'd send my way every time a problem fell into line and worked. And then we began having these intense conversations, maybe about how hard it was now that Hobart was off at school—and I pretended to like the hell out of Hobart—or my dating difficulties or some other utter nonsense that was a guise for letting off all that teenager angst that playing basketball or blowing on the French horn just didn't seem to cover.

When she asked at lunch time if I could give her a lift home after some school civic foolishness we were involved in, it gave me three hours to plan it all out. After dreaming about the possible outcome of this historic conversation for months, I realized I didn't have any idea what to say. By three-forty, I still didn't have an idea and would have been desperate if I hadn't been so jacked up over just having her walking out of the school with me. When the time came, I would know what to say.

She slid in and curled into the seat, letting one shoe drop and putting her leg under her, all smiles and relaxation. Then I tore out of the parking lot leaving a rooster tail of dust and gravel. Alice Ann went for the arm rest. "What's wrong with you?"

"I don't know, I just like to drive fast every now and then—get it out of my system, you know?"

She didn't. She looked like she didn't even know me. And for a while, as I concentrated on slowing down and keeping the car in my own lane, we didn't say anything.

Then I said, "Well." She had her shoe back on now and both feet pushed firmly on the floorboard. I decided it was too late to comfortably turn on the radio. So I counted to fifty—it was only five miles to Alice's house—and started talking. "Hey Alice Ann, have you ever noticed the way Hobart gets that little sheen of sweat on his face even in the winter? How he's always going over his face with his hand-kerchief?" It occurred to me that I'd found the reason why his glasses kept coming down his nose, and I told her so—on account of the sweat. "Have you ever noticed or thought about it?"

"Yes," she said.

And then I told her about the phys-ed class I'd had with Hobart when he was a senior and still hadn't passed his gym requirement because he had asthma or something and now he had to take it or not graduate despite being at the top of his class. And what a klutz he was, which was true. But I left out the part about how I always contrived to be on the other side to cram the volleyball down old stumbling genius Hobart's throat.

Still she said in a quiet voice, "Why are you telling me this?"

"Why? Why? Because," and I took a big breath, "Because I am crazy about you and have been since the first time I ever saw you." And much more of the same that mercifully I can't remember.

"Stop the car. I can walk from here."

I pulled the car over in front of somebody's house and reached over and locked her door and kept my fist on the lock button. A snoopy woman came to the window and stared at us sitting there. Alice Ann was solid stone—her chin jutting out like she was Nefertiti herself.

"Why Hobart?" I yelped when why not me was what I meant.

"You'll never know." But she let me drive her the rest of the way home—at least she didn't make a move for the door when I took my hand away from the lock and eased the car back into the road. In her yard, she just said, "Oooogh," jumped out and slammed the door.

"Oooogh? She didn't tell you to go to hell or nothing?" Weasel said. "You don't have a chance. Let me fix you up with something for the prom." And he did with Sherri Pozo who could get out of her bra faster than any woman I have ever known. But it still wasn't that much fun.

I got up enough nerve to apologize to Alice Ann on the next to last day of school, and she gave me a big hug and said did I understand? I told her yes.

I let myself in the house and sit down in the living room. Back in the kitchen, my parents are talking over top the noise of the television. It's the news of the world ground coarse or fine. For them, I suspect nothing Dan or Roger can say will have quite the impact of the questions of loaves of bread and quarts of milk and the paid on accounts and cash sales versus the charges and bills. The store hangs on the precipice and Mom and Dad can't understand why. Where are the customers who want their meat cut to order and helpful cooking instructions written on the butcher paper, the ones who appreciate a tip on a recipe, who appreciate service? All gone off to Kroger's and A&P chasing specials—chain store tricks. And how much gas do you think it takes to run all the way to Bluefield to save four cents on a can of peaches? Like the commentators on TV, my folks don't have any real news either.

Still, I wait and listen. It's good to hear them saying it all again because for them, getting up every morning, opening the beat-up gray doors and making too little money for their hard work is all they need to know about who they are. Despite their complaining, they are strong and sensible and satisfied. They know people are funny—they won't buy mustard at ten cents a jar, but jump at it at two for twenty-five. There's no understanding the buying public; but yourself, that's another matter. Me too; right now I'm thinking about dying Roland and what I ought to do. It scares the piss out of me just like when coming down the stretch in the fourth quarter of a tight ball game, the coach would call time-out and say, "All right, let's get it inside to Dog now." After that, whether the shots dropped or missed, I had no control over them. I was like a maniac or moron, not to be held responsible for my actions.

It's time to present myself in the kitchen: "Well, it's the world traveler," Dad says and waits for me to fill in the details.

So I sketch out the Roland Barker story, and Mom grows red rimmed around the eyes—the very idea that we, that is *homo sapiens*—have come so far, that Roland will get up and walk out of that hospital blessed with his sight and everything. "They say there aren't any miracles in the world any more, but what can you call this?" she says. "It's not the same kind of miracle as in the Bible, but God moves in different ways in different times." Let's compare miracles. My favorite is when once in a stinky tent out on the Sinai, God showed Moses his hinder parts. It's from little clues such as this that we learn what He really thinks of us.

"And Weasel," I tell him, having excised our meeting of the night before out of my previous debriefings, "I saw the Weasel."

"Huh," says Dad, his strongest condemnation of anybody. What is wrong with Weasel? I'd like to know. After all, my dad was fond enough of him when he was throwing me passes. It turns out that in addition to his adventures in the drug trade and his interest in scarcely post-pubescent girls, Weasel doesn't respect his mother. "You should see her," Mom puts in, "up and down the street all day looking for him so she can have some money to do her shopping." I do see her, worn to a nub of a woman, since she was that way even ten years ago when I'd go around at two on a Saturday after I'd finished delivering the orders and find the Weasel still in bed. He'd raise hell when she got him up, hang a padlock on his bedroom door and demand a meal. He was a picky eater.

"He'll end up in jail yet," Dad predicts darkly.

Dad may be right, but I'm hoping there is still some good in the Weasel. "Well," I say and make it stand for an apology. Besides, I have to get going. Soon it will be time for the reunion, the dread purpose of my trip east, though it seems as the time gets nearer that, in truth, I am as Weasel said, dumber than Barker, driving a thousand miles so a married woman who might show up will autograph my program. Is that why I'm here? To tell you the truth, it's another question I haven't gotten around to answering.

Mom senses I'm holding back, sitting at the table where my place hasn't been laid. "Shouldn't you be getting dressed?" And then, "Where are your other clothes?" meaning the ones I will wear to the reunion. But I have none except the sackful she has ferreted out of my room and washed thoroughly. "What do you plan to wear?" she says in genuine distress. I shrug and she goes straight up to the hall closet and finds an old tan checked summer sportcoat and the brown slacks that go with it hanging where I abandoned them for the less formal attire of the liberal left. Mom assures me that a little work with the iron is all they need.

What can I say? I accept the sportcoat and substitute a pair of cords, worn in knees and seat but fresh from the dryer, for the slacks. "It's your reunion," she begs but not so hard as to get me to back out of the sportcoat. For this I am sad, how the years have worn away some of her power so that now she's so ready to compromise.

A few minutes later I present myself shaved and showered with the coat and cords, my sockless sneaks, socks having somewhere along the way dropped out of my summer wardrobe. I have this white polo shirt that I found draped over a tennis net with Charlotte Country Club on the breast and a little golf flag on a green shaped like an artist's palette. It gives me the air of studied casualness, something like I'd imagine the America's Cup crowd throws on after a hard day on the yacht. If I just had a fifty-nine Caddy with a few superficial dents, I'd be right. "The coat looks nice," Mom says, pleased with what little she could do, "I hope they let you in."

The place is *Tony's*. Twenty years ago people would have called it swank with its blue tinted windows running all across the front, the fake rock siding around the door, blue floodlights stuck around the shrubbery and the name, *Tony's Roman Garden* in running neon script. I climb out of my car and the feel of the damp pavement in the strange parking lot, the tension of my mission, make me feel like I did when we went to away games. Coming into the other teams' gym, we would just step inside the door and line up against the wall in our white shirts and skinny ties and black varsity jackets and scowl until we were sure everybody had a chance to take us in. Then we'd saunter down the visitors' sideline and stomp up the bleachers to the top row where we'd watch the JVs with hostile indifference.

Remembering something of the feeling of invincibly hot shit, I go on in to where I find the class in the specially reserved banquet room. I see them first, looking from the way they are standing in loose linked circles like they are just out of a country church and are waiting around for the brief moment of polite conversation before everybody piles in his car and goes home. Except they have drinks, and of course this thing is scheduled to go on past midnight. Then they see me and suddenly everybody turns and opens outward. Where there were circles now there are overlapping fans of people. Mainly they look. Will my own classmates, the ones who voted me the sportsmanship medal, turn me out because I have holes in the toes of my sneakers? No. After a short silence, suspicion turns into embarassment and somebody, George Hager, my biology lab partner—his drawings were almost good and he had a gift for cutting things up—comes forward, calls my name, shakes my hand and tells me drinks aren't covered in the cost of the meal. I thank him and ask him how he's been. "About the same," and I think that even though it's been ten years, he's not lying. "Me too," sounding not too convincing. I do look the same, long and skinny in the neck with my Adam's apple bobbing. But to them it's too much like "Not of this Earth" where your neighbor has been made off with by a flying saucer and has been replaced by somebody who looks exactly like him. But those in the know aren't fooled for a minute—there's something about him, this alien Martian agent, that just ain't right. All night I suppose they will be asking me questions designed to trick me like, "Who did you sit behind in tenth grade English?" when they know I was in the front row.

Then a woman steps in and leads me over to where I must sign in to some fairly complicated book that requires besides my name and address, answers to a series of questions. Such as, "Your personal philosophy?" suggested, no doubt by a housewife who has self-helped herself to happiness from the book selection at Kroger's. I flip through the back pages to see what others have written and find, "Charlie and Jack Daniels, my best friends," "Christ is the answer (often)," "Lead with your left," "Smile!" "If you have to ask, you can't afford it," "When guns are outlawed, I'll be an outlaw," "God loves you and I love you," "I (little heart drawing) ceramics," and a short testimonial for Mary Kay cosmetics. Frankly, I admire these blurbs of simple truth. If ceramics can bring you inner peace, salvation, better orgasms, isn't that the same as sitting around saying Om and listening to your ribs shake? Maybe I'm even envious. In my own blank, I write N/A.

When I can dawdle no longer at the table of old snap-shots and yearbooks, I go back to the group. They're having what some might call a high time. Everybody's buying these crazy drinks off a top-forty radio play list: piña coladas, Margaritas, Tequila Sunrises, even the Baptists who hold them uncomfortably in those little cocktail napkins with our school and class year thoughtfully imprinted on them. Who knows when, years probably down the road, searching for a ball point pen in his sportcoat pocket, somebody will pull out that wadded napkin and remember, what?

A little guy in a hound's tooth sportcoat is talking in my ear while I pretend to know him, "They took up the Indian head."

"Oh." And seconds later I understand he means the Indian head in the center of the court. I used to step on his nose at the beginning of every quarter for luck.

Remember that. I've seen a gym floor in the process of being refinished. They have this mammoth sander, bigger than a commercial floor polisher, that just eats away at the layers of varnish down to the lines that mark the boundaries of the floor until it's blank as a tabletop. I picture the Indian, stern bastard with a full head of feathers, getting more ghostly with each pass of the sander.

"We're thinking of getting together a fund to have it put back. What do you think?"

"I think I'd like some plain whiskey in a glass the next time that waitress comes back by here."

"About the Indian head?"

"Not interested."

Now I've insulted him, this roly-poly little coal miner, red in the face with me and from carrying too much salami in his dinner bucket. But I like the idea of the Indian head being gone just now. It makes it easier to remember. "I'm sorry," I tell him and fork over a couple of bucks. And through my offering of money, I find these people opening to me. "So what are you doing now?" they ask me.

I'm starting to see the evening stretching out in front of me as a minor trial, somewhere on the scale between a visit to an old absent-minded relative and a trip to the dentist. Alice Ann won't be here; it's not her kind of event any more than it's Weasel's. Nothing to do but brace myself and wait for the sit-down dinner. Put a spread of food in front of people, even total strangers, and conversation takes care of itself.

Just as the social hour is breaking up and we are moving to the banquet tables, Alice Ann, a brisk woman in a pumpkin-colored shirt dress and sandals, no stockings, rushes in to save me. Her face is harder than I remembered, or has gotten that way. She glances around, eyes flat like she's looking for the one empty seat on a bus full of strangers, and I remember she was never that popular, committing the sin of being too self-contained. When she spots me, she comes to the table and forces herself a place, grabbing my hand in both hers, a Chrissy Evert backhand grip.

She is only a high school mathematics teacher, a real ruler cracker you can bet, mean enough to scare the lust out of any high school boy's heart. But not mine. God, she is tan and taut, and I'm feeling the near nausea of want.

There's this slab of cold roast beef in front of us now and some mashed potatoes and green beans. "Canned," Alice Ann says picking at hers. "This meat is raw. You can have it," scraping it on to my plate in the old cafeteria style, and while I'm not hungry, I eat it just because it was hers.

"So what about you?" she says, pushing her plate away and turning in her chair to face me. Now I feel naked and exposed—the antic nature of my wardrobe seems to have lost its charm. I can feel her disapproval but it's still mixed with a spirit of generosity—there is an explanation to all this, right? I keep eating, finding it hard to swallow, but easier than the truth. Between bites I tell her as little as I can about the crooked stair I've traveled. What sounded like the adventures of Steve Roper and Mike Nomad to some coal miners hungry for a little excitement, now sounds exactly like what it is. My jobs of house painter, warehouseman, mill hand, gas station attendant are the ones for the drunken and undereducated, the kinds where nobody asks you for your employment record and nobody expects you to stay on.

"You've certainly been around," she tells me. I thank her with a smile and she suggests, noticing the way I have of wiping my sweaty hands on the calves of my pants legs, that maybe we should go where we can talk more comfortably. So she gets up and leaves the reunion with me tagging behind like I'm going out to the hall with teacher to be told the hard news that I'm flunking. Passing the bandstand, I lift a bottle of the grocery store champagne from the ice. "Hey," somebody says, but I keep it.

She lets me drive her car, a red Volvo as befits the wife of an electrical engineer who has gone off on his own into private consulting as Hobart has. I find the solid weight of the car and the hard but perfect steering a boost to my confidence. With a car like this I might actually amount to something. "Where to?" I ask her.

"You decide."

So I start for home, for old Powell's Bottom, seven miles by Pinnacle Rock and Bramwell.

"I haven't been over to town in ages." I give her a question with my eyebrows that she catches in the dim dash light. "I don't know. Why really? Everything's dying—I'm sorry, your parents are still here, I know—but it's true. Hobart says the whole town will go from the carbon monoxide, just sitting on the street with their engines running."

"It's peaceful and gives you a rosy complexion."

"That sounds like you," she smiles and that coupled with the hum of the defroster fan makes me feel snug. Am I supposed to? "I wondered about you," she goes on and I just wait, "It's not what I expected. I mean, I knew you would be different, I wanted you to be. But not like this."

"What's this?"

"Don't. At least you'd be a math teacher like me."

"It was the calculus. Every day it was something about using a pipe to fill up a swimming pool on time." I give her a big smile to tip her to the joke.

"Dog, I thought we were friends."

We were, now are we again so soon? "I made some mistakes, that's all."

She puts her hand on my long knee poked out over the shift knob and gives it a squeeze. "Me too."

The Pirellis Hobart's thoughtfully provided at seventy-five dollars apiece stick to the roadway and the nightime wraps itself around us. I'd suspend us at this moment but too soon there are the railroad tracks and Powell's Bottom. There are faces behind the windshields of all the cars parked up and down the street, but we can't see them through the reflection of the lights. "See?" says Alice Ann. Right now somebody might be asphyxiating. I wonder if Weasel could be one of them. Then I turn up the valley road to the high school. Alice Ann pushes her weight against the back of her seat, bracing herself. But she must have guessed we'd end up here when she let me drive. I ease up to the back of the gym, cut the lights, kill the engine.

We were on the subject of mistakes, I believe. "Is it Hobart?"

"Yes."

"Why don't you just leave him?"

"It's not so easy. You think he's strong, don't you? He is in a way. But he's depended on me so long he's forgotten about it. If I left though..."

With her quiet, there's nothing but the sounds of our awkward shiftings in the seats and the pings of the cooling engine, our only sense of time passing. "You tried to tell him about this?"

"Yeah…no, not really. I do cruel things. I pick at him. All I have to do to get him started is to remind him he's from Powell's Bottom. It always ends with him giving me something."

"Like this car."

She gives me a hard smile. "Like this car." I know she's mad now, except she says, "Do you know what I did that day, the day you gave me a ride home? I cried about you." And now she cries again as an authentic reproduction of how it must have been—big air gulping sobs. I watch from my side of the transmission hump, but wonder why. There are just too many variables and I was never good at those kinds of problems. She gets herself under control pretty quick, takes a long breath and says, "Let's walk. I feel like a walk."

We get out, me dragging the still unopened champagne, go up the bank to the football field, saved for phys-ed and summer softball, football being long extinct in Powell's Bottom. We stand for a minute on the edge of the broad dewy field. Alice Ann slips her sandals off and wiggles her toes in the dirt and grass.

"Why don't you take yours off too?"

"Mine stink."

"It doesn't matter, you could leave them here." She's forgiven me.

I do, tying the laces together, flinging them over the goalpost. We walk up and down the field, around it. She bumps against me, and I slip my arm around her waist and leave it there. Without talking, we go on until we're weak in the knees and clammy with sweat and my other arm feels like it's getting pulled out of its socket by the bottle.

By silent mutual consent, we go sit in the ruins of the bleachers. I get the top off the bottle with my pocketknife; it doesn't even spew. We drink the cheap stuff down in long healthy swigs.

"How did you keep from getting married?" she asks me.

In my crowd the subject never came up. "Luck."

We start kissing, just nuzzling around at first, then warm, full wet kisses. Maybe we are drunk, but I don't think so. I put my arms around her and pull her against me. Occasionally, we rest our foreheads against each other, look and smile. That's all. I don't even have a hard-on, though I'm sure I could manage it at the appropriate time. What we've got now is something that can't be alloyed with sex. There will be time for that later.

"Alice Ann," I tell her when I am resting with my head in her lap, "I'm looking for a woman that shoots straight and don't ride sidesaddle."

"You are such a fool." And hearing her tell me makes me all the more certain she is the one. "We'd better get back to the car." So we do, across the field where it takes me three tries to get my sneaks down. It's late and I still must do my duty by Roland Barker. She drives.

As we idle outside the restaurant, I sit with one leg out the door and say, "I'll come and see you tomorrow."

"I wouldn't like that," she says.

I take a folding chair and sit it beside the bandstand where the Eldorados are now performing. Just now they're doing a mid-sixties soul set, the kind of music Roland and his band never much bothered with, not enough guitar in it, some Tams or Temptations stuff where the whole band does a little dance step in the chorus, except the Eldorados are white and going to pudge. Still, I listen. I want to prepare my appeal and having nothing whatsoever to say, I put myself in the hands of this band of accountants, school teachers and disk jockeys who take up their instruments on their days off and sound like it, too.

Nonetheless: Sing, o muses, of Roland Barker and his red guitar, and assist me to tell how, never out of the doghouse with fortune and his fellow man and wife, he sunk even lower still, until, funny how time just slipped away and all his kids call another man daddy, he stands on the edge of the wide world where love and fame come to nothing more than a hole in the cold, cold ground. Maybe he'll reach the happy isles, but I doubt it.

Because despite all the talk about rambling men, he wanted nothing so much as to sit in the front porch swing, pick a little and have a true loving woman for him, a good loving man. Heraclitus tells us the world is all fluxed up, and I believe it. So for Roland, it's time to catch the Detroit Special out of Santa Fe. Make him a headlight on a northbound train, he's going with Hobo Bill on one last ride to Byzantium and turn into a speckled bird on a wire to sing the song the robin weeps for all the lords and ladies there.

Shouldn't we go down to the river—take your rocking chair—and give him a little send off now that he's almost naked and done turning cold? He'll shake hands with our mammas when he reaches that beautiful shore, won't he? But I'd just like to say if you believe that, then tell me if it wasn't God who made honky-tonk angels, who did?

Saints standing in God's holy fire, bless me, curse me now because to tell you the truth, it's only money we're after. Just enough for Roland's silver-haired daddy to dress his boy in white linen cold as the blue moon over Kentucky and to have himself a bottle or three of store-bought liquor. No point in asking for more than you have hopes of getting.

In passing my time in this innocent way, leaning back in my chair, thinking, and watching my happy classmates dance, I manage to piss off the lead singer of the Eldorados. Here comes Tony himself who demands to see my name tag which may surprise you to know is right here in my coat pocket all the time.

Well, he's sorry as hell and offers me a drink on the house that I'm inclined to accept. Tony's a pretty good guy despite his pointy-tan, almost pink, shoes that lace together and dyed inky hair. I watch him gesturing with his hand in the vicinity of his ear to the lead singer, this one hitching up his sequined cummerbund, as if to indicate I am perhaps an inebriate or mildly demented or a combination of those two, but otherwise harmless and unlikely to take the stage, seize a mike and attempt to sing along with "You Send Me." Never mind, this guy still gives me a sour look as if my presence in the field of vision is enough to ruin the whole show. I stay; it's the nation that controls inertia that will rule the universe. I don't know what gave Dick Tracy the idea it would be magnetism.

Finally the band limps through a gummy version of "Under the Boardwalk" and promises, with that cheap heartfulness that must be hard to muster at eleven o'clock, to be back shortly for one more set. I'm on.

When I step up to the dead microphone, I'm greeted with jeers mostly, the feeling seems to be that I had more than my share of the champagne. But I make a Nixonian gesture of reconciliation, arms open wide into limp peace signs. "It's about Roland Barker," I say.

There's laughter from back in the dark and smoky banquet hall. "Dumb ass," which could easily apply to either of us.

But wait, I know these people. Just because they've joined the Church of Jesus, been baptized in the blood, bought a ranch style house up on the hill and have a wallet full of the kids in their Sunday clothes doesn't keep me from remembering they got those kids in the back seat of the old man's car, would have denied them, too, if they could have found somebody else to put the blame on, which doesn't mean they didn't try. "We all make mistakes," I tell them.

"Amen to that."

"We're his friends." Having started off in that direction, I might as well keep lying, ride on through the laughs and sneers. "I wonder how many of you know the true story behind Roland's little accident." Pause and dour expressions while I scratch around for what's next. "Last spring," and I see an Appalachian spring full of red bud and dogwood, "Roland first began to notice something was wrong. He felt weak, he dropped things, got dizzy at work." I'd like to conjure the ghost of Lou Gehrig but my detractors see it otherwise, suggesting anybody would feel that way if they drank the cheap shit Roland did. "I wouldn't know about that," I say, stepping around it. "But anyhow, he went to the doctors. They weren't able to tell him a thing. Then he went up to Charlottesville for a solid week of testing, no Blue Cross, no UMW medical card, no nothing." Pause again. "You can imagine the cost. It wiped him out, him with a wife, two children and an old father to support. The doctor called him into the room where they give you the bad news, the one with the desk and the diplomas, and said '. . .Mr. Barker. . .you have. . .MS.' " Sure, MS—their radio spots call it the number one crippler of young adults; it got another one. I hear a few gasps of incredulity, or sympathy. The tide may be turning.

I clasp my hands in front of me, wring them a little and go on, "Yes, he tried to take his life. Under the circumstances, what would you do? His wife's left him but still wants her alimony and his daddy, for years supported by Roland, has no way to pay the mounting hospital bills. Roland's on life support systems. Picture it, today he can't even push down the strings hard enough to make a chord on his guitar, not even E-minor. And one by one, little by little, each and every part of his body will stop working. He'll piss in the bed, they'll have to feed him through a tube. But his brain will still be in there working. They can't keep him on those machines for months, years without some kind of payment, can they? Maybe he'll be taken off for somebody richer, somebody with pull, somebody that those who don't know him will consider more deserving."

Whew, hard work and horseshit with no indication I'm on target except a creeping stillness in the room. "I went to see him today. It would make you weep, a babbling stickman. He doesn't even know his daddy. But here's the sad part: In his delirious state, he still breaks into song, the words come out to "Rock and Roll Music" and "Maybe Baby" and he jerks his arms spastically trying to finger a chord, to pick one of his licks.

"Remember with me if you will. Look at this stage and see Randy keeping the back beat with his foot pedal and chewing gum. Pecker and Darnell struggling to lay down the rhythm. And Roland, so lost in his music he was past pain and embarrassment. We laughed at him, didn't we?" (I hear

140

embarrassed laughter.) "I only hope now when he sings out those tormented lyrics in his dreams, 'You can knock me down, step on my face, slander my name all over the place, but don't you step on my blue suede shoes,' that he's beyond pain in that moment, too. How can we ever know?

"You're wondering what, if anything, we can do. Not much. Except maybe make a gesture, a gesture to show that outside the narrow walls of Roland's hospital room, somebody cares. A gift of money then, to demonstrate our concern. A little bit might go a long way in convincing a busy hospital staff in these days of cost-analysis that we won't let Roland, our friend, be forgotten.

"And remember, 'Whatsoever you do for the least of my brethren, you also do for me.' " That's in the Bible, I think. I smile a broad, all lips smile and wipe my brow. Meanwhile the dead room slowly comes back to life as the Jaycee types hustle around dumping uneaten brown-and-serve rolls out of the bread baskets and start them around. There are those present who know everything I've said is the most shameless Bible salesman flimflam. As long as the surface tension holds for a few more minutes, I can take the money and put a couple of long grades and blind curves between us. Besides, it's not exactly stealing.

When the loot finally comes to me, stacked by denominations, all faces aligned as per good businessman procedure, I gather myself for my last act in the spotlight. No greedy leering and fingering the bills, I tear a sheet out of the reunion program—the one reserved for autographs—and wrap the money, slip it delicately into my breast pocket. "Thanks, thank you. I know he'll appreciate it in his own way. And I promise you it'll be used wisely," and so on as I begin to sweat it for the line I can break away on.

The damned Eldorados save me. Coming back inside, smoke still trailing out their nostrils, they've got to wonder what happened to the party. In the interest of helping them get the festive mood reestablished and as a sincere memorial to Roland, I go up and request "Wooly Bully." They don't know it.

At least it gives me a chance to make for the door except that I get intercepted at the last moment by Sherri Pozo, who sticks a stricken mascara-smudged face into mine and cries, "You don't even remember!"

"Sure I do, Sherri."

"Well, dance with me then, I'm divorced and willing."

I tell her that maybe it wouldn't be right, considering the sad circumstances of my errand. She's going to pout, so I compromise myself and say, "Maybe a slow one."

It's late when I wend my way home. My mom all innocently asleep would have been proud of my extemporizing; she always thought I would get the calling. My dad, though, would be watching the ground, certain it would be another example of the one-hand-over-the-shoulder basket catch, perfect save, the ball lonely and white against the grass, for the moment unnoticed.

I count the money, well over four hundred dollars. Generous assholes when push comes to shove. I'd be proud of them if I knew they weren't already. I peel off one hundred in fives and tens and put it in my wallet, then put the rest out where mom will see it in the morning.

Then I'm off to bed. Now's the time I regret how I left it with Alice Ann. Wondering whether it would have been better in the long wet grass of the ball field or in the reclinable buckets of the Volvo, I let the salubrious effects of the alcohol carry me away. Tomorrow's a busy day.

III

Damn. Eleven-thirty and I'm hungover, too.

Mom found the money. "I would have thought your classmates would have given more. It isn't like coal miners don't make anything these days. And it's for Roland."

"Yeah? Well, I had to compete with the Indian head." I wanted to get down to the kitchen early and talk to Mom, work off some more guilt before taking off. But even with a healthy dose of vitamin C, bacon and eggs pumping into my system, I can't fend off her indignation. I hide in the want ads. It's not that I'm looking for a job or anything; I just want to see what's out there, get conversant with the market. "The Indian head contingent got there first."

She's soothed a little, but wouldn't you think, she thinks, the people would have wanted to throw the Indian head money right on top of the rest? It's not so much her faith in mankind—down at the store she would have lost that years ago; even Roland snuck a honey bun into his pocket when he could get away with it, ask Dad—as that she wants to pick us up by the scruff of the neck and make us be better despite ourselves.

Some have tried and fallen short of the Kingdom, others have never made a decent effort. If you asked her which category I belong in, I wonder what she'd say? And she doesn't even know I'm leaving yet.

"Today? Now? You just got here."

"I have to get back to my studies," which qualifies as the biggest whopper since my arrival. There's enough white heat beyond my paper shield to make it spontaneously combust, taking me along with it. Why is it now I feel curiously distanced?

Let her batter me if it makes her feel any better. "Your father and I never asked that much of you. We never asked you to be anything in particular. But be something."

"OK."

"What, then?"

I take down my paper, carefully fold it up into a quarter page and lay it out beside my plate, a shotgun ad offers a sporting chance at a sporting price. "Mom, would you be surprised if I told you I probably won't finish my degree?" She looks at me, eyes big but empty, waiting for the rest. "I don't know. I'm just way behind; I can't think of any good reason why I want it."

"So." I've affirmed the worst, but at least I'm honest and doesn't that count for something? For her, I guess. For me, I would be happy enough to think up a lie good enough to believe in. "What will you do?"

Sit on a rock and think for starters. But it seems like I've done that for a while now to no good end. "I'll have to think about it on the way back."

She just shakes her head. We both know there's no point staying on here where the business at the store slowly dries to a halt. If anything, I should be ready to honor and comfort Mom and Dad in their old age. "You're as bad as Roland," she tells me. "Only he never had the guidance at home. With you, it was different. But here we are the same, neither one of us knowing what the fuck's going on. He was a little more musical about it, that's all. "Don't worry," I tell her out of obligation to take the high road after the bad news, "I'll get it straightened out."

"You couldn't prove it by me," she says.

At the door she gives me a kiss on my tall forehead; I have to bend to take it. It's not like we haven't been here before, but I can't help hearing the plaint in her always last question to me, "When will we see you again?" as if this time the answer might properly be never.

"When I have good news for you."

"Christmas?"

"Maybe. I hope." I take up the pack and the dry cleaning bag with the plaid sportcoat and brown slacks. Mom offers to touch up the tail of the coat with her iron.

Maybe I should have let her.

My car makes a mighty effort on the steep climb, but it still needs some help from my creative shifting to get to the Barker place. I set the emergency brake as I look out the rear-view mirror at the blue cloud breaking apart on the hard drop behind me and decide to chink a rock under the wheel as a precaution.

Then through the two rotten posts that are what's left of the Barkers' gate. Nothing much has changed. The two vintage Plymouth coupes still hulk in the side yard with their

144

hoods thrown off in the high grass, one ruined engine block with the heads missing that as a kid I wanted to get ahold of and dissect fully is close by. Then, the rest of the yard was full of the rusting artifacts of Roland's childhood, a swing set with the candy cane paint still visible in patches, overturned tricycles and pedal cars. All I knew was I never got any neat stuff like that.

"Groceries," I holler and go in the back door, letting the screen bang behind me. Inside a couple of long legged hounds snooze on the dirty kitchen floor. There isn't much furniture, two straight back chairs that must migrate around the house. There are dirty glasses, empty liquor bottles, catsup bottles with caked gook all down the neck. Still, there's no old man.

I stick my head in the front room and see him asleep in his clothes on the same couch the old lady died on, twisted up in an old afghan. His mouth's thrown open so I can see the black spots of rot on the few teeth he's got left. I guess I could wake him. Instead, I go over and lift the needle on the old suitcase style hi-fi from where it's probably been bumping against the record label the better part of the night. Even the label feels warm—Kitty Wells on an old discount bin label.

I take the money still folded in its reunion program and put it out on the kitchen table, weight it with one of the fuller bottles. Over the mimeoed names of our classmates, I print in heavy blue ink, "For Roland in his time of need."

My dad loads me up with a box full of every non-perishable commodity he imagines I might need. In many instances he's wrong. I have, for example, a gallon of bleach in quart bottles from previous excursions of this type. On top of all this, he adds a bag of hard, barely ripe pears, my favorites. Then after forcing all this into my back seat, he runs back in for one last thing—a case of recycled motor oil special ordered from some wholesaler. He grins as he throws it in the trunk on top of my recap spare.

Mostly I'm left with his handshake, thick in its strength and simple staying power. He waves as I pull out, then ducks

145

back in the store where things hold together through the force of his presence as much as anything else.

Although the mailbox is anonymous black, this must be the place. Besides Alice Ann's red Volvo, there's another one in the drive, a little silver and gray limited edition coupe. I decide I don't like its looks, pull in the driveway, hoping Hobart has yet another car, and break up the happy Swedish family. My Datsun will leave a little oil spoor on the pavement; I take some pleasure in thinking Hobart will be just the type to get bent up by a smudge on this otherwise flawless house and lawn. Flawless, not exactly right, though. Despite the round healthy boxwoods, the thick bermuda grass, something's wrong. No flowers for one thing. The house for another, which is two stories with porch to match, these clumsy columns stretching up to a narrow roof, brassy outsized carriage lamps hanging by the double doors.

Alice Ann meets me in tennis clothes, still damp from the court. "You ruin everything," she tells me. Hobart asks from the living room who it is, then rises to meet me as I follow Alice Ann in, smiles, judging me. "They used to call you Dog, didn't they?" he asks, faking the absent-mindedness.

"That's me."

"Well, Dog," he seats himself slowly, catching his good flannel slacks just above the knee and hiking them up. Alice Ann has made him a gentleman genius: that matching gold Cross pen and pencil in his white oxford shirt, skinny gold watch tucked under his generous cuff. No hairy unseemly ankle as he crosses his legs, folds his hands, comes round to my interview question, "What is it you do these days?"

"Graduate work," I say over this phlegmy catch I suddenly develop.

"The ascetic life."

Hell with this. He's still the same clumsy bastard I hit on the head with the volleyball. Besides, I covet his wife. "Yeah, ascetic, not to be confused with fairy's or monk's."

This, he thinks, is funny. He laughs a pseudo-hearty laugh; I smile along with him. We sit there suspicious and

146

ignorant. I guess I could ask Hobart what the chances are he'll stick his finger in some high-voltage socket while he makes his consulting rounds. Fortunately, he gets up, shakes my hand and makes his excuses. He's going to clear out. I wonder, does he know? Was he expecting me, and if so, am I so transparently a hurting case that he can leave me with Alice Ann?

No matter, he's gone. Alice Ann says, "Coffee?" and then goes off to the kitchen to get it together. The furniture in this room with its matching wall-to-wall is the more tasteful shade of green found on the face side of folding money. The tables are low slung, modern, from the same neck of the woods as the Volvos, I'd imagine. The walls, though, are empty. Here, Alice Ann's sense of what's what has failed her. (The outside excesses I pin on Hobart.) You can't put framed calendar pictures up in a hundred-and-fifty-thousand-dollar house. But what do you put up? These blank walls make me feel much better. In some small ways I'll be able to take her in hand and teach her.

She arranges herself on the other side of the coffee table (I could hurdle it, I suppose), checks my preference and pours. Then she waits. Well?

"I came to ask you why?"

She pushes a cup my way and invites me to take some of the dippy store-bought coffee cake she's got to go with it. It occurs to me that she and Hobart live the life where such high-tone munchies are necessarily always on hand. Bridge club: It's my lead; Alice Ann plays the dummy. "Why you cried when you got to your house."

Blank look.

"In high school. Like you were saying last night."

"Oh God, I don't know. That was ten years ago."

"Try." It comes out too much as a plea.

She slides back into the comfort of the chair, chews her cake, "How much do you know when you're eighteen years old? You got to me, that's all. You got to me and I didn't know why. Maybe I loved you more that afternoon than I could ever love Hobart—those things you said about him weren't too nice, by the way; he couldn't help it—or maybe it was that I just sensed that you were more my type, emotionally, I mean. But I had already promised Hobart. Back then I kept my promises."

"And now?"

"Bluefield is a small town. It's not Powell's Bottom, thank God, but it's still small enough. I'm lucky Hobart's an engineer; he never believes anything unless he sees it."

Now's the time to jump. "Alice Ann. . ."

"Don't."

"What?"

"Say it: You love me. You want me to run away with you to that place in Arkansas. You can't offer much but there will be love."

I wasn't going to say that exactly. But what if I did?

"Dog, you see this house and my car and can imagine the clothes in my closet and the tennis club and the vacations we get to take on Hobart's salary? I like all that."

"Well," and I can't get much farther, casting around for some demonstration of how, while I couldn't come up with all this, I could at least buy some drinking glasses that don't have Looney Tunes stenciled on them. Sell my bicycle and use the money on a Penney's suit and some short-sleeved dress shirts, drop out of the grad program and take a job—insurance, encyclopedias, aluminum siding, Amway—and *poco a poco* work my way up from whatever the modern equivalent of the mail room is until I own the place, not to mention a professional sports franchise? Of course, there will be plenty left over to keep Alice Ann in designer tennis togs and radial tires.

"Admit it. If I said yes, you didn't even have anything planned."

She's got me there. "No."

"Hobart was right, you're an ascetic. You don't even mind going around in your dirty tennis shoes and blue jeans. You don't mind that terrible car that could break down any minute. Your life is in your mind."

Fatuous bullshit of the worst kind isn't it? The sad thing is five or six years ago I would have bought it. Now I can only wonder, does she think I am so easily taken in, or has she been? "What about last night?"

"Let's call it a mistake. At the next reunion, we'll laugh about it."

I eat my slice of cake, swallow down the coffee, dust the crumbs off my lap to the floor. "I don't think I'll be there; neither will you." Time to clear out.

"I'm sorry," she says.

"There's nothing to do about it is there?" I'm already standing.

"I mean last night. It was special to me, too. And my fault. You didn't match the picture I had of you. Who knows, if you had, I would probably be wanting to run away. But for one night, I could pretend. You were sweet; most guys wouldn't have handled it that way."

"Thanks." Because she's right. Because to pursue it any farther is to face up to facts: Alice Ann is a rich bitch and I'm a what? Who did write the book of love anyway? Whoever, he was full of shit. We're better off screwed up in monophonic. "Last chance," I tell her.

She takes it as a joke. "Going back today?"

"Now."

"Take care of yourself, Dog."

She shows me out, closes the door behind me. The car feels sluggish under me. I'll take it out on the by-pass and burn some of the oil off the plugs and wait out the time until I meet Weasel. Alice Ann? She's going to go back to her money-colored couch, start to gather up the coffee things, then sit down and cry. I know that; I've learned something. But as to the reasons, they're as lost and distant to me as they would have been that first clumsy time I struck a glancing blow to her heart.

Weasel is waiting when I park on the lot where the Old Moose Lodge used to be. Smoking and giving me a leer that says he's had a little chemical help in getting himself up for the crime, he slides out of the van and locks it. "Let's get drunk afterwards," he says.

"OK, but listen, Weasel," I'm feeling dishonest because I tricked him into coming up here, but I still need his help, so I go on. "Listen, I think there ought to be a little change of plans."

"Say it then."

"I think we ought to go on and kill Barker, put him out of his misery."

Weasel grins and throws away his cigarette. I think it's a question of money, but he says, "You had it figured out this way when you asked me yesterday, didn't you?"

"Mostly," I tell him. All of it except whether I could actually go through with it. That's where Weasel comes in. With him along, it will be harder for me to chicken out.

"Figures, because the other way was just too damn crazy. It just didn't seem like you."

"You still like the money then?"

"Fine. It's easier this way, huh?"

It is? I kind of wish I was high myself as we go down the street and then around to the back entrance of the hospital where they deliver the bottled oxygen and the burger buns, where a couple of orderlies are out sitting on the wire milk boxes taking a smoke. They look at us going through the Positively No Admittance entrance like it happens all the time. It does. It's still offical visiting hours so Weasel and I don't look like we don't belong once we get into the halls. Weasel, I suggest, doesn't even look the assassin—the rubbing alcohol, the piss and puke, the covered trays and carts that nurses push around the halls with God knows what hidden under those damp towels—organs? Extra, superficial parts of people going to the incinerator or wherever—putting everybody into a daze. Get in that room, chin up to your friend or relation and get the hell out. We're all on missions of some kind.

"You know where he's at?"

No, I don't except that it's a safe bet that he's out of the intensive care unit by now. "Come on then," Weasel says. He knows where he's going.

We head up to the second floor, down past the private and double rooms, the nurses' station where the staff is too harried by visitors fraught with concern to pay any attention to us slinking along. It's what you might call the indigent men's ward, empty except for a couple, three wino-looking guys, one busted up from a fall maybe. The others look like they're most likely just drying out. But with the tube on, they give us the once over and let us go on to a bed with a screen around it over in the corner.

It's him. "Hello Barker," says Weasel leaning over right into his empty face.

"Weasel!" Roland says with a little squeak. Here the little fucker is with one foot over the edge and trying his best to pull the other behind him and yet Weasel still has the power. "It's OK, Barker," Weasel goes on, "Dog is here. We're going to help you out, at least that's what Dog says." Barker is flopping around on the bed trying in his weak way to make an escape.

"It's me, Barker." I put my hand on his arm real easy, and he stops his squirming. "We're going to help you, understand?" He only nods. "I'm going to have to unhook these tubes. Weasel's going to cut off the oxygen for a little while, You know what's going to happen?"

"Yes," he whispers.

So I make to unhook all this rigging, get right up to it and: How does it work? Where to start? What if some kind of monitor is spliced in and an alarm goes off somewhere down the hall?

"Here," says Weasel bumping me aside, quick with his hands on the tubes, the hissing bottle of oxygen. Then he steps up to Barker, who's already, it seems, starting to run down, and watches. We can't just let him die, even Weasel senses it. Grinning like a vampire, he puts his hands to Barker's neck.

"No. Let me. You hold him." Weasel clamps on to Barker's puny biceps with his big smart hands, and I wrap my long fingers around his neck and wring what little life there's left out of him. He doesn't struggle.

Weasel puts everything back like it was; we walk out of the ward, down the same back stair and out the delivery entrance. The orderlies are gone, but even so it has been something less than a perfect crime. Still, we're home free. Depite what might easily be suspected, even noticed, nobody will care enough to bother checking it out.

As soon as we get back to the cars, Weasel lets out a crazy cackle and says, "The Stadium Club."

I follow him there.

The Stadium Club shares its space with an operation that claims to sevice all domestic cars and most foreign imports, that offers a smiling bear's solution to your alignment problems, and doesn't bother to haul off the rusting unsalvageables that collect out front. Maybe that way there always seems to be a crowd inside. I try not to see any omens as I park my car with the rest of them. We all like to be with our own kind.

Hence the Stadium Club, the little nook of a room where, when this was a full-fledged service station, you went to pay your bill, buy a pack of cigarettes, a girlie car deodorizer. These are Weasel's kind. And to see them, you would know how true Dad judged him. Swivelled around facing the door, there's a guy in a leather cowboy hat, satiny shirt with galloping stallions coming at you. In his face I read headlines about bodies of chubby preteen girls found in shallow graves. He and Weasel know each other, you might call them business associates. He's got a hellacious stereo out at his trailer, Weasel tells me I've got to see it. And then as my general introduction to the crowd, Weasel sets them up. After all, it's my money.

Somehow I had thought after the deed was done that Weasel might feel bound by the camaraderie of the outlaw class. But there he was, sidling up to me before I could turn off my engine. Grinning, head cocked, he was hoping I wasn't going to be tasteless enough to make him have to ask.

I pulled out my wallet and counted out the dirty bills, slipped them to him in a tight roll before I got out of the car.

"I knew I could trust you, Doggie."

I told him I appreciated it.

The guy running the place puts the jukebox on free play, and Weasel punches up every Ol' Waylon selection. He suggests we party down until the place closes and we do. There's nothing but beer, but at least we are buying the better labels, Miller and Michelob. Deciding it would be wise to get drunk, I work at it pretty hard, lose track of my beers.

I'm not drunk enough though, was more lightheaded the night before. It's not what you're thinking. It's not Roland walking his guitar across my brain like Chuck Berry. He's out of it now, off to more attractive surroundings unless in some perverse spiritual way, neatness counts.

It's me, isn't it? Pretty soon even the Stadium Club is going to shut down, and I kind of like it here with the moth-blasted stuffed beaver that sits on his haunches up there beside the Dr. Pepper clock. The counter guy sees me looking up—the grease-yellowed menu's there too—and comes over. Maybe I would like some food? No, but it does remind me of the machine outside the Ashland station when we were kids. After playing ball all day on the court behind the Baptist church, we'd go down there and one at a time slip up to it and punch it just about where the heart would be if there was such a thing in a pop machine and a Dr. Pepper so cold there would be ice in its neck would come sliding out like a baby born. I never liked Dr. Peppers any other time.

My bar man thinks it's just drunk talk, looks at me sad, and then down the stubby bar where Weasel is poking our easy rider in the chest with the butt of his half full bottle. They're laughing as the beer sloshes out onto the floor between them.

"Known him long?" meaning Weasel.

"Way long."

"How you figure he got this far without getting himself killed?"

"He's working on it."

But this guy doesn't know what I'm talking about. "Sure. He's going to get himself shot, stabbed. I just hope it doesn't happen in my place."

For Weasel, I'm thinking, it won't be that easy.

Weasel buys a six to carry with us when we finally get put out the door. I should travel and tell him so.

"It's early yet."

"Where are we going to drink it then?"

He just gets me into the van and drives across the way into the big stadium parking lot over by the historic loco-motive, fenced in to protect it from the less civic-minded, where basketball courts and goals have been laid right over the parking spaces. We're at center court now, looking down into the infinite possibilities of the passing lanes on a good three-on-two break. I watch Weasel from where I might be trailer. He dribbled high, over his waist, but without turning the ball over, just driving it into the floor, pumping his knees high like a halfback. More often than not, he'd want the dribble in his left hand, his free one drawing your eyes like a magician's. After a while we all knew not to look at it, just the ball, otherwise you'd miss the pass when it came—arrived really, floating in front of you like a cloud, a pass so soft a baby could handle it. Or maybe after coming almost upright at the foul line, he'd shift to just one right hand dribble and be through the defense and in the air.

Weasel feels it too. His hands dance around the smoked up interior, punctuating our talk about cars we'll never own, women we've always wanted, but on a truer path of their own.

"Shoot some?" He has the ball, an almost grainless Voit rubber job, stuck away in the bottom of one of his liquor cabinets back in the pleasure end of the van.

It might be the damp mountain air, it might be me, but I feel like I'm moving, breathing in an atmosphere of molasses. Weasel reminds me that I always was slower than a Sunday shit. But what about him whose grace has gone all mechanical, brittle. He skitters like a crab in his street shoes, under my lazy arm, flips in a reverse lay-up, all eye, no touch. I don't have much either, never did. For me, it was sheer force of practice. Now I turn like a dinosaur in the pivot, hoist up my arm for a hook and try without much luck to locate the rim, focus and shoot. Air ball.

We fall into a little one-on-one, pulling the ball out behind the foul line and trying to drive. Weasel on his plastic soles slips and slides, almost has me beat, throws up what he can to keep from walking. I use my butt to back him into the lane, then can't make the shots anyhow even after tipping some back three or four times. "We suck." We laugh about it.

"Let's play some points," Weasel says.

"You're too drunk. Free throws."

Weasel belches and gives me a hard look. "You know I'll beat your ass."

"You're drunk," I tell him again, thinking all the while he might be right.

"Don't do it." I do.

We play for dollars, it seems the only respectable figure now that we're big boys. Weasel goes first and makes seven out of his ten. I can't match it. Mine are crooked, flat. "What are you aiming for?"

"More arc," Weasel keeps saying, honestly trying to help. I get three, drop four dollars back. And when the cops come by, scaring the mortal piss out of me, but surprisingly, friends of the Weasel, it seems, easygoing and funny, advising us to play for a good long time—I'm down thirty-three dollars. We're going to have to; without the money, I'm not going to make it back to Arkansas.

I keep hoping I'll be able to use one of Weasel's cheap digs to get me ragged enough to concentrate on these damned throws. How many do you reckon we've thrown up there, two or three hundred? I am sick to death of pumping my arm. I even go oh-for, but Weasel only makes four himself. He tells me we'll cut it off as soon as I get down forty. I should be grateful.

It isn't a question of wanting it this time, is it? What can I do, go creeping back into Powell's Bottom and put the bite on Dad? Alice Ann? She could filch it for me out of Hobart's walking around money. Nope, just no place left to go. I have to make some shots and I do. Give Weasel credit too, he's about sick of the whole business, besides drunk on an empty stomach. So after maybe three hundred more shots, I pull all even. "Oh hell," Weasel says, sitting against the bumper of the van, "You're even, let's quit."

"I say when now," I tell him. We quit after he owes me three dollars.

"Mr. Clutch," and he gives me the money. There's nothing to do now but shake hands and walk back across the parking lot to my car. "Come back to town, you could leave your car here and stay at my place and nobody would even know."

"No."

"Diane? The one with the tits?"

"Can't"

"Well, don't say I never gave you nothing." He gives me ten dollars and watches me back to my car, waits to make sure it cranks. Then, with a three-tone salute, he leaves me.

It's maybe an hour before daylight. Nobody but the dogs out this time of night. I take it through the dew damp streets, thinking to pick up the by-pass off Maryland Avenue and then get the Interstate. It'd be the safest thing, given my indelicate condition.

But when I pull up the ramp to that new road that's been sliced against the edge of the mountain, I think of the old one, old twenty-one that takes you over the mountains: East River, Brushy, Big Walker with its snake pit and observation tower where you can see five states. I find my way to the turn-off for East River, pull off long enough to reach under the dash and flip the toggle activating my goose. It goes before me casting a luminous sphere of blue light. I pray it protects me from bad spirits, ghosts and vampires. I've begun the long and twisting climb over the mountains. As Weasel might tell me, it's early yet.

Frank Soos grew up in Pocahontas, Virginia and was educated at Davidson College and the University of Arkansas. His essays and stories have appeared in *Writers' Forum, Quarterly West* and the *Cimarron Review* as well as other magazines and journals. Along with artist Ken Woodward, he is editor of a book of essays, *Here Is Where We Live: Artists and Writers on the Alaskan Landscape,* forthcoming from the University of Washington Press. His short story collection *Unified Field Theory* received the 1997 Flannery O'Connor Award and will be published in 1998. A recipient of individual fellowships from the National Endowment for the Arts and the Alaska State Council on the Arts, he teaches English at the University of Alaska. *Early Yet* is his first collection of stories.